The Preachers On Manic

By Paul Outhwaite

D.M. Productions

The Preachers On Manic Street

By Paul Outhwaite

Copyright © Paul Outhwaite, D.M. Productions 2005

This edition first published in 2005 by
D.M. Productions
PO Box 83
Coulby Newham
Middlesbrough
TS8 0FX

British Library Cataloguing in Publication Data
A catalogue record for this book is available from the British Library

ISBN: 0-9537461-5-1

"Honesty is a fine jewel, but much out of fashion"

Thomas Fuller, *Gnomologia*

POST-APOCALYPSE, POST-MODERN, POST-IRONY, POST-HASTE,
I WORKED AT THIS NOVEL IN A HASTE,
AND PARTLY A HAZE.
OF IDEAS, FIRING OFF.
FIRE. TO SHOOT, TO KILL.
FIRE AND PASSION,
SOMETIMES WORDS AND IDEAS GROW FALSE UNDER THE SCALPEL OF RE-
DRAFTS.
BETTER TO SPIT IT OUT AND LET IT STAIN.
SO, HERE ARE BULLETS.
IMPULSE.
ANARCHY.
DISORDER.
HERE, THERE, THE MAN – THEY FEAR YOUR INNOCENCE BECAUSE IT IS
RIGHTEOUS AND PURE AND UNSHACKLED BY WEARY REASON.
SO, FROM BIRTH THE POISON SLOWLY SEEPS – MOCKING NAIVETY,
FORCING CONFORMITY, PURGING THE SPIRIT.
THE DRUNK HUNCHED ON THE CORNER, IN PANTOMIME BABBLE, IS MORE
HONEST THAN TONY BLAIR.

FIX ON CLEAN, PURE AIR AND INHALE. DEEP. PREPARE. LIGHT A FUSE.

1
WHERE WE'RE FROM

Looking at the year 1979, at the loaded numbers squeezing to change, I am aware of history's indentation. Margaret Thatcher was just a name then, from a collection of words breathing asthmatically from our increasingly dated television, the sounds divided unevenly into the consciousness of the four figures inhabiting our front living room. I'm the least receptive, my years still single, my wonder still impressed by the idea of 1979 changing to 1980: An eight and a zero; a whole eighty. Fantastic and futuristic, enticing possibility; the sound was fattened by accumulation, ready to burst percentage bubbles.

It took time for the digits of the year to be integrated, for them to seem normal in the school exercise book, squat in the thick space heading virgin pages. Each new imprint offered a fresh start, all other work and disreputable marks subject to a scorched earth policy. Neatness and order were self-imposed by a personal aesthetic coloured by some subconscious hope that this composition would be the shining example of what I could offer. Or perhaps it was a fear; that at any moment some belligerent force was going to invade the classroom and take away the work that I was engaged with, systematically gathered to save or convict me.

Whatever the motivation, once the purity of the page was scarred by symbols and signifiers, and that first inevitable mistake blotched perfection, the old order was restored. Crosses marked the graves of the moments when I thought I had mastered mathematical tasks or scientific equations, whilst in English ideas were too often flying ahead of conventions, leaving behind a smudged reality. Red verdicts took praise to the autopsy chamber, quartered by caveats, and divided by measured comments coldly ruling on spelling. As if that could survive the blood and thunder of my howling imagination!

1980 was the year that my birthday cards were emblazoned with two figures; with a heroic *10* in monumental font, pronounced like epitaphic summary. Pictures of cowboys, of football kids and sports car drivers, of cakes and candles, balloons and boxes; verb-riddled, one-dimensional heroes with ethnic, ill or alien skin, animated the imagination, triggered shots at scenarios in my future life, but were realised most strongly in the present of my invention.

We passed the parcel, between the hands of those whose names were not just the monikers of convenient acquaintance. Here were friends, some felt more intensely, but all bonded by the lifeblood of infancy, so that each name was part of a character integral to the joy of the game, the mood, the occasion. A circle of twelve pawed and paused, heart-beating rhythms anticipating a jolt, excited by the roar for silence.

Ripping at the skin of the parcel, hopes were soon dashed as music squeezed the oxygen once more. Closer to the prize, rhythms of songs were subsumed by a hungry chant yearning to win that which would be given for free by the end of the evening when the rapture was dispersed into cold winter air, the smoky breath fragile in the doorway, creeping back into the light as hands meet over a threshold. They skate away with tales to tell, reliving favoured moments shorn of minor slights.

I always remember the parties on Manic Street, not through specific details but through the regularity with which one was held. And what remains most truly are the beginnings and endings of other people's parties: that moment of knocking on a door, waiting with card and present, waiting to enter something magical – the balloons, lights and music, crowding to be cosy, boiling up an irresistible expectation of indulgence amid the gathering of like minds all eager for the evening's games, getting high on laughter. Then the cool walk out into night when the party was over. It felt as though the world had changed.

This was a childhood clattering through doors that never tugged back when you yanked to get out. Locks and bolts only snapped and cracked at night, when I lay with possibilities and listened to incomplete circles of sound. Passed the next two rows of houses, a path devoted to the light-heated and leaden-footed auditioning for the night with half-remembered tunes soaring away from memory.

"We can't go on together with suspicious minds..." found vocals on shaky ground, way out to sea, stressed and emphasised as the affectation of tragedy. Tommy Madden was affecting a yearning to be taken seriously, his chorus joined by Danny Bertram as a means to gently mock George Lewis.

"Come on Georgey, give us a song. You're the king, the king!"

"I'll give you a clip, Danny boy."

They would coax something out of him, something brief and hushed as they came into Manic Street, and they would both be less inclined to ribbing as he absolved the fragmented night of sin. He took his place under the street light outside his home and bowed to his appreciative friends.

"See you below," someone always said when they parted.

George Lewis stepped into the thinking-of-you kitchen light, a pocket of welcome and protection in a downstairs closed for the day. Although these nights had grown less frequent and were less about an intoxicating future, the drink now fuelling nostalgic drifting, George's return home preceded a reassuring routine. He poured himself a glass of water, pulled up a stool, lit a cigarette and turned through the local evening paper, only half-interested in the stories he might have missed earlier that day. His mind always drifted, invariably to a sixties summer and Mississippi, Memphis, Tupelo, a series of road signs and sunsets, storms that X-rayed the sky, clouding dirt tracks as the band travelled to unheralded towns to play their music. He reminisced in rhythms, formed pictures in his head through clumsy lyrics, making the fires of youth smoulder until his cigarette slouched out ash under the force of his finger.

Upstairs, he took a piss, washed his face, cleaned his teeth, put the towel in the airing cupboard, slipped out of his ageing clothes and pushed open a door to see his sleeping son. A kiss on the boy's cheek prompted a shuffling of position followed by a deep sigh, which let George into innocent dreams. He moved to his daughter's room and did the same, lips gently touching the stability of sweet dreams. Into his own bedroom, a bedside lamp illuminated his wife Helen, a book loose at her hands as she slept. He kissed her, removed her glasses, put paper between the pages unread at her breast, and turned off the light, reassured that regret wasn't diluting the nostalgia.

Every day is the end of an era. Hindsight may often be rose-tinted, but regret and loss are as powerful as the warm glow of nostalgia. This town, much like any other town where community and society actually meant something, got left behind somewhere in the 1980s. It didn't feel that way when the decade began. Then, I was still protected by the soft tissue of innocence, but soon I would see the gradual erosion as a sudden abrasion, and by then it was too late.

I remember 1980 for the death of John Lennon and a sadness that had no basis in history, but young as I was there seemed significance in death, its arbitrariness all the more shocking when sweetened with the sentimental tunes being played to my impressionable emotions.

Eric Morecambe also died in 1980, and despite no gratuitous prompting of sentiment, he felt closer not only to me, but also to the people around me. There would be no more Christmas television specials shared with the family. For the first few years, repeats satisfied, my memory not yet bold enough with history. Then, the teenager in me rejected the old-fashioned without just cause. It was not until my mid-twenties that I felt the loss most acutely, for it was only then that I could pinpoint the warmth of an era – of childhood – and feel regret at how change had less brilliance and vibrancy.

Let me colour. Summers were long and pure; winters were deep with invigorating snow. In between, there was a race of some sort. At ten years old, I was roaming up and down Manic Street on my Chopper, jumping off kerbs like Evel Knievel, oblivious to anything but the worlds created in my imagination, looking up to my brother Mikey, who got his first motorbike that year and started working at the coal mine, following in my Dad's footsteps, but only until he had the means to make real his dreams. My father, Eddie, had worked there since he was a teenager, inheriting the "job for life" from his own father. He didn't much want either Mikey or I carrying on this tradition, telling us all the time to "get an education, boys. Be like your mum, get reading and don't show your face underground." My mother, Bella, was once a union secretary, which was how she'd met Dad. She'd given it up when Mikey was born, becoming instead a skilled mother and housewife, her perpetual motion of worry, energy for games and organisation anchoring the family into a solid oneness we probably took for granted. Not Dad though, frequently invoking mother's philosophies and acknowledging her rightness during our upbringing.

Mikey leaned on an adult-halving brick wall at the front of our house, one of many stages and pulpits dotted along Manic Street: "Listen Petey, this little baby means freedom. I'm not tied to anything. I have no restrictions. I can go anywhere in this country, or I can put this bike on a ferry and go to Europe. Always make sure you've got freedom. Freedom is a road seldom travelled by the multitude, brother."

 Some words hit, some words missed. When Mikey's monologues got bogged down in technical babble, numbers tumbling, I just looked up and took every figure as a measure of the bike's power and Mikey's vitality.

When alone, I was amassing my own words to bridge the gap between the real and the inexhaustible, neatly plotted fantasies I scribbled in my room. I liked to find new words, exploring the stories behind their meanings, but sometimes even just the sound of the word could attract my use. I learned a new word that year too – "redundancy" - when my uncle and some of dad's friends lost their jobs because of "cut backs" at the steel factory.

Manic Street was amongst a collection of terraces bleeding out from the sea front, interrupted by the management of road markings, bending around the back of the high street and being fed from the old industries of coal and steel, beating and pulsing further down the coast. Both were the town's major employers, clothing and feeding the population, invigorating the cells from dawn 'til dusk, taking in and releasing bodies to fuel homes and meeting places.

These workers would right the world and preserve dignity over fluffy beers in the thickened corners of familiar pubs. They profited from friendships inherited, from the terraces that had housed their mothers and fathers, the bonds shifting only slightly with the sophistication of a semi-detached. When Dad came home, he dragged in the grime of new tales to tell, some embellished for my amusement, some censored by the ceiling, dulled by walls as I lay in bed, watered down the next day in Mikey's re-telling.

Mikey, or Michael to my mum almost all the time, was my hero when I was ten. He could make me laugh, energise my imagination and ameliorate doubts with his infectious positivism. Even if mum and dad had had an argument that chilled the house, Mikey could conjure an act to warm the soul. He got into some scrapes, my mother's chastisement noted yet never puncturing my image of him as tough and cool. Bruises that occasionally surfaced never revealed victory or defeat, and though he was embarrassed to be wearing such markings, his nonchalant indifference to them suggested to my impressionable self that he was untouchable; his participation in some imagined battle enough to show his bravery. He had energy in abundance, fuel to his big plans of saving up money from working down the mines, and eventually having his own motorcycle shop. He talked about it to me often: "You see Petey, I'll be an expert and all the famous bikers will come to me for repairs, or to make their bikes better. You see, when you're your own boss, you are free. If you want a holiday, you take it. Me and you, we'll be behind the bike championship winners."

Hard to tell him, I wasn't that interested in motorbikes. I liked the way they looked, liked the sleek aesthetics of the Matchbox replicas I pushed around patterns in my bedroom carpet, imbuing the supposititious characters who rode them with predictable heroics. But, beyond that, I would have been bored with the mechanics of mechanics. Mikey had a passion all right, and that's what hooked me when he was unwinding his dreams and anecdotes, but as a career, it didn't touch me.

There was a group of them who hung around driveways along Manic Street – Mikey, Chris Atkins, Matty Bellison, Khleel Khan, Paul Chadwick - kicking around the future and returning to the past to embellish and amuse. Those who passed by would often stop to feel some of the warmth, throwing an anecdote into the pot.

Danny Madison was just over a year older than Mikey. He lived near the end of Manic Street, pretty close to the sea front. He popped words and boxed around plans and ideas: "We don't seem to matter any more. Ordinary people don't have a voice because all that politicians offer are options, limited ones at that. People voting out of fear, too scared of losing some money to tax, too scared that some other party of tabloid-invented demons will come to imprison them in a gulag." Danny was born to this, his angular features and crew cut sculpting his face with polemic precision.

"Capitalism will fail this community. It'll destroy the idea of community. Thatcher's policies are all about profit, about cutting loose the weak, because they'll be the losers, they won't make the pound to fund the tax cut."

"Danny, I know mate, but you need to relax a bit," advised Mikey, a disarming smile and easy-going manner truncating the rant. "They don't care about us up here, but that's fine, we have plenty of fight and spirit. We won't be destroyed by anything any politician wants to do."

"That sounds a bit like a cop out," replied Danny. "Apathy isn't an option."

"I thought this was a democracy," Mikey shot back, converting the mood to laughter.

Danny too had self-mockery in mind with, "Come the revolution brother, for the good of everyone, you'll do as you're told." He sat on the wall. "Look at them. Remember when that was us?"

"It's still me, Danny."

"Yeh," added Chris. "We've just changed push bikes for engines. We're still as mad as them. Got a few more worries for sure, but we can forget all that on open roads."

Larynxes were straining with the screeches, improvised on bends in pursuit of acknowledgement. We were going around the block, our block, in monotonous motions within the race without end. We were so consumed that we transcended the mundane reality and imagined our frames being filmed, watched, cheered and admired by a multitude on the peripherals. We felt none of the twitching and fidgeting of adulthood, somewhere behind the curtains or tangled in a routine. We were heart bursting, biting the air voraciously, unwilling to be smothered by time. There was no sound in our ears but the signals from our imaginations, so that the calls to return or participate in a schedule were deliriously babbled and subsumed in the mass of everyday living.

But we did notice the adulation from the kids on the street – the home lane of Manic Street alive with those willing to indulge the fantasy or even be taken in by it. So Mikey was roaring on, audible only when his words had weight:

"One lap to go."

Simultaneous with the embracing lustiness of disparate animation, a few houses down there was a group of toddlers sonorous with glee, drawn into the action as senses ran loose. There was Lisa Burnham, her left arm waving as her right arm let the feet of her doll get dirty in the gutter, dragging it around, looking for salvation. She led the wave of excitement, contained in pure sopranos at a threshold of participation, delirious in their hesitation, vicariously thrilled to suppose it might soon be them. Some of the boys – Justin Carson, Sean Patrick, Gary Orton and Jimmy Best - crossed into virginal worlds with their willingness to run alongside for as far as the air let them dare.

Johnny Young rang the glory bell to announce his presence, lost the pedals and lost balance around the bend at the foot of Manic Street. He tumbled and grazed and felt like crying, but didn't. Half a block to go and the race wound down, heads turning to see what Jimmy had done, gasping at a pain tongue-tied by originality, speechlessly rising to the surface of his skin. In the ensuing discussion we turned our curiosity into a question of honour:

"Nah, it's not fair if Jimmy crashes. We'll have to race again."

"Yeh, that's why I stopped an' all."

"Me an' all."

"And me."

Johnny was the same age as me, Paul and Andy, so we were engendered with a unity born of fearful fates, which just missed us by chance. The younger ones too were breaking with caution, halting their machines out of some kind of respect or fear. Two of the older racers carried on with Marcus Bowles lording it over David Traynor.

Johnny was okay, now curious at the capacity of his own body to blemish in various shades and contours, as inelegant calls bounced unfinished harmonies from doorways, announcing teatime, with an impatience that sizzled. The group dispersed from the scene, but maintained the moment with good will and a bond learned from flickering heroes, sure that tomorrow would be just as exciting and new as they swerved homewards around the parallel prams of Liz Byland and Brenda Maines, lips shaping to announce mimicked noises of screeching car tyres suggesting swerves out of control, but controlled by imaginations looking at themselves in celluloid.

The two mothers were small-talking passed their new baby's real or imagined beauty and cutesy ways, into the fundamentals of a domestic ritual that rattled with tittle-tattle, tongues loosened by bites of water washing down the days that crowded them:

"Our Donna's left her fella again. Sez he's too busy going out with his mates. Well, y'know what they're like. Anyway, she's staying with us for a bit."

"'Til they kiss and make up again. They're worse than Burton and Taylor them two."

"I know, but it's nice having her around, helping out."

"You don't stop do you? If I'm not running around after Jenny, I'm round our dad's, making his dinner, wheeling him down the bookies."

"What about your Brian?"

"He's working overtime most of the time. Ey, he's heard there's gonna be job cuts next year."

"Aw, don't say that. That's the last bloody thing we need."

"Ah don't think they'll let it happen mi'self."

"Here, he's George Lewis, ask him."

George Lewis, trailed by puffs of cigarette smoke and the dust of the day, leaned in from the spinning world: "By, you've got two crackers there. Hello darlings," he said, peering in, seeking to shrink his wave to enter their world, before turning to the mothers. "Are they good for you?"

"Ooh, most of the time," spoke for them both.

"How old are they now?"

"Coming up a year in two months," replied Mrs Maines. "Hey, George, 'ave you heard about jobs going at the pit?"

George toiled back his quiff and felt the dust clog: "That's what they say. They haven't reckoned on the union though. Can't see them letting it happen."

George Lewis had been working at the pit since he was eighteen. In those twenty-seven years, the camaraderie and solidarity of the men he worked beside had rosy-ed his outlook, kept him as the benevolent head of the family, got his hi-fi updated every five years and got him and his wife Helen a ticket to America in 1970 to see Elvis Presley in concert. He was thankful without being complacent, but an ethos of reciprocated care and optimism had steered his life to the age of forty-five with the healthy glow and hearty humour of someone at ease.

When he got in, he kissed the memories that had brought him to this place, fell out of the stiff dirt clothes of the day and washed the grime from beneath his fingernails, then shared with Helen the anecdotes that had let them breath in the day. Until the coffee cup was empty, then he soaked, opened up a routine and cut it loose, flicking on the turntable for some old tunes that seemed like yesterday.

A forward motion, the needle skating into his past, he laid on his bed, revolutions of thought and the miming of his fingers squeezing keys into sound. Nostalgia junky, he mainlines most nights, an aural anaesthetic to numb the aches and pains that have grown more regular as the past has slipped further away.

He is not alone. It's a conscious comfort to have walls breathing from one to the next, to know that the sounds inducing reverie are drifting ghost-like into the corners of next door, having effect, prompting some thoughts and images, some change of mood however slight and ephemeral. Maybe someone is singing along, able to ignore the row that is burning itself out further along Manic Street. Every emotion is fading, windows inhaling and shutting out the wind as it follows a concluding arc of achievements noted in yarns. Tails invariably name sources from somewhere along the street, coloured by characters known to the storyteller, threads frayed from repetition, detailed out as they journey to another source.

Tired goodnights fix on kisses, tasted through the ice of a salty gust, purified by the cold as steps lead away too, shifting to work and grit, taking a pulse from the earth. A night switch flicked, an artificial light, sweating the soil for the subconscious' black stuff, blessed by a rain of dust fogging thoughts, merging thoughts, and diluting the toil through haphazard banter. Shouted above mechanics, inflated by clotting air, it touches everyone, reciprocating chortles coughed about confines, delivering sin from the pit.

Every day roughens the skin, marks experiences that take the body further from God, years marked out in contours that leave an imprint of those individuals passing through, caught up in the morning scurry of litter to the sea. A tinny symphony, a crumpled wheezing; the rhythm of disposables blown head first onto the wall at the sea front, where their internal squabbles go nowhere, but to salute the flapping flags in spasms above, whip-cracking time against the amnesia of progress.

The flags were all waving in 1982, flying high outside the Conservative Club, saluting commerce in shop windows, rightly royal upon ordinary homes. Even the tabloid cut outs slapped up on Manic Street twitched with fervour.

It was during the Falklands War that I felt a most perceptible change, initially thrilled by the prospect of battle: a glorious display of the military hardware that I had been gluing together for some years, the possibility of heroes and the seemingly clear cut distinction between good and evil. Somewhere also was the sense of unity it brought: the talk of school friends, the talk of Manic Street, and the talk of a town hitting the mainline of a nation surrendered to disappointment, now gluttonous with ideas of faith and murderous god being on its side.

"Those cheeky bloody Argies won't know what's hit 'em. You don't mess with British soldiers. Some driveway philosopher trotted out, "I'm telling you son, they don't stand a chance against our boys," rallying round the preachers on Manic Street.

"God be with them," was said with a note of caution, but in it there was the vile trust in a selective deity.

Nonetheless, there were enough old heads around whose questioning I heard from coat tails, whose animation and vigour I felt, prompting me to dig a little deeper in newsprint. The contrast in military strength was the first thing to give me doubts. Then to see on the television news the youthful faces of those Argentine prisoners of war, their uniforms tatty, their equipment old, their helmets filled with lice. No time to be drunk on an age, the dictators they couldn't question extinguishing a time to be reckless, sending them off to kill for a distorted patriotism.

Bill Harris, at number forty-two, paused on his way home to share tobacco thoughts with a friend from way back in the union days. A few years short of retirement, Bill was still working hard at preventing further redundancies at the pit: "I see bloody flags everywhere, Albert. You'd think the queen was coming to the bloody town. It's a distraction is all it is, make people forget about what's going on at our own doorsteps. They can afford to spend millions of pounds sending armies to war, but they can't keep working the industries that help families put food on tables. It's all wrong. It's just more money for the fat cats and who cares if somebody's son, somebody's daughter, somebody's father or mother dies. The people waving on glory don't know anything about war. They wanna have a dead body dumped in their back yards, that'll change their minds."

"Glories in slaughter," chimed one of the preachers, sounding like an incantation, calling up the ghosts of wars and homemade tragedies. "Glories in slaughter," like a town crier shaking nametags to the sound of pebbles squeezing tight underfoot.

"Glories in slaughter," proclaimed waves of concurrence, cheering them home from their campaign to whip up support.

Bill Harris had fought in the Second World War and been awarded several medals, which he kept in a box, but rarely talked about. His conscience carried a wound for thirty-five years that would return a pain without warning, each palpable recollection not diluted by time and serving notice on the notion that the barbaric images were only alive in infrequent ruptures of present security. Who had he killed? What was that soldier's father doing now? Had his life been cut short too? Had Bill's thirty-five years of family life been mirrored by some prolonged anguish for the mothers and fathers of unformed enemies? The son he was so proud of often seemed to disappear when he brought his family to visit Bill and Katherine. Bill would watch, think vaguely about different routes of life, and feel as if his son were being cut adrift, merely an image in a dream. These hazy ideas indented his sleep, acute prompting rolling over and twisting the obscure presence of lives extinguished. What of his daughter, who would one day cradle a baby with unconditional love? Would she ever recover from losing the child in battle? Could he ever offer her the comfort of reason?

"And we probably sold them the weapons that they're going to kill our boys with. This Tory government is no different to previous governments, selling weapons to tin-pot dictators around the world. How can you rationalise selling things designed to kill?"

"It's all wrong," emerged the refrain from Bill's audience: kicking, screaming, vulnerable and needing. "And they've got these nuclear weapons that can destroy the world hundreds of times over. I guess they just want to make sure there's nobody and nothing left alive. They cost millions and millions, but they say we need them for peace. It's barmy, absolutely barmy."

"Hi Bill. Hi Tommy. What's the big debate?" asked Danny Madison, returning home for a break, invigorated by ideas from nearly two years of University.

"Hello Daniel," came from both old men, for they had got too used to the name that Danny's mother and father used.

"What do you think of this war, then?" asked Bill.

"I don't agree with it. I think Thatcher wants it though. She doesn't seem too interested in diplomacy anyway. Get ready for Hate Week, eh? *The Sun* newspaper will tell you how to think. There's a rich man peddling Thatcher lies and feeding it to the working classes and those scrambling towards the middle. It's a rolled up newspaper, slapped against the head of the working class if they try to think too much. The Argentines are foreigners, so they must be evil. No, don't think. Whack! Here,

here are some tits to distract you. Now you can start hating and don't try to understand."

"Glories in slaughter," retreated, hard-bitten and sound-bitten, sinking through the cracks of sentences jostling on pages recording histories, descending to a footnote never to be dredged.

Drowning in patriotism, some of the preachers on Manic Street felt comforted by the flag, vigorously waving for the braves they wanted to know and love.

"Our boys have done us proud," came from an age of less ambivalence, before overuse and misuse cast it as cliché. Said here, the preacher seemed more intent to retrieve a notion of togetherness, the sounds of her words circular and reciprocal. They were our boys: our "us" could unify and breathe and open and encompass, but of late such an idealism had been ageing and become vulnerable, disappearing without fight up the arseholes of politicians.

Liz Byland was retrieving dead words from a battlefield, trying to breathe life into "They fought for a right cause," but caught in the crossfire of Right-leaning propaganda as lives were slipping away from Manic Street to find work.

Len Marks went alone, whilst The Bellisons shifted a family and left skeletal the home that had been held at the end of Manic Street by the sum of its parts. One night, the symptoms of shattering glass brought out a speckle of lights, spotting the darkness as doors yawned questions and a unanimous conclusion.

"Tearaways," said a preacher, the obsolescent words hanging heavy on the shrugged shoulders of those preachers too weary for solutions.

"I'll phone the police."

Muttered agreement signalled the prelude to a retreat. The next day the Bellison house had a wooden left eye. A couple moved in, let light in briefly, before moving out. The Bellison home was soon blind.

Down at our house, Mikey was loading his things and preparing to move out, but only to a flat a few miles away, nearer the town centre that he was to be renting with some friends. There would be a few less tall tales.

Mind you, apart from an absence on evenings, he seemed to be around as much as ever, still clanking tools on the driveway before heading off on a jaunt along the coast. He'd always wanted his independence, never cared much for being told what to do. He didn't like to feel trapped. I guess that's why he liked the bike so much.

With Paul and Andy, we were spinning wheels towards the horizon, pushing back our boundaries, blurring into images to take a hit from the here and now. There is a mutual history with us three, but there is no immediate awareness of what it concludes. Neither is there a mapped out future. We are diving into the now, pawing out the present, embraced in a pulse of the senses. We want to explore what we have never seen and we have no need to leave a mark, for we are clattering the present, shaking up and waking up, unfettered by a need for meaning.

We cycle onto the pier, dismount and push towards an end, wooden beams aching by time and motion in a fitful sleep against the snoring, sloshing sea below. Moving towards the end, it prolongs a feeling like our regular world is being left behind: the push-button, digital symphony of making ends meet as a means to an end fading away. We are scared of our imaginations, capable of optimism and belligerence in extremes, warning us of a collapsing structure. But we have no rationale for death so we dismiss it, moving closer to the end, to the edge of life.

There exists only us three. I have the drinks, Andy the sandwiches and Paul the crisps. We share as we instil the scene with scenarios, given life by clichés and stereotypes. We are poised on the big *What If?* And we are eager with fast-paced potboilers, all of which "could come true." We excite each other with "Imagine..." preludes, shrinking the elaborate to fit with possibility, until it is emboldened and boundless, alive with "might". We are carving our memories around this town, opening up its pores with every run, jump, kick, skid, leaving all we did as "Did!", "Did!", "Done that!" upon its shedding skin.

"Do-wah diddy, diddy-dum, diddy-dee..." joined the crowd at the Labour Social Club where George Lewis was re-living his glory days, rattling the organ, squeezing in his rhythms, accompanied by a band of 1950s teens unwilling to let go of history. The crowd that danced knew the names of the band, intermittently shouting out support and friendly insults. George on organ, Pete Thornby on drums, Dickie Chadwick on bass and Ray Young on lead vocals and guitar had been sharing riffs and rhythms for several decades, though much less than they'd once done. For now it was a hobby, something that did more for them than could be counted in payment.

The nostalgia was lacquered, sweetened by a present that seemed less certain, where identities were being eroded from all sides. Their soles were trying to wake spirits from the past, muscles twinging for a sense of the character they once were. Treading on romances, glances, missed chances and all the raggle taggle of other cuts from history, they were dusting off the dead. Through the joins in a floor embalmed with beer, living diaries peep. Archetypes in black and white rear from record the memories they are dancing to inhabit. Smoothed and soothed by hindsight, they are already drifting away, too light and fuzzy to re-awaken real feeling, but just enough to leave content. Enough belief seals the vents in the Labour Club, so that a feeling remains in the tightened air, circulating the crowd to anaesthetize the senses.

By the end of the evening, the body is lumbering away, curling homewards and inwards, and dragging visceral thrills away from the Club. The "goodbyes" and "goodnights" fall heavily from an exit, whilst inside temperature falls, making ache the sinews of wooden legs scraping the shell, retreating to order. "See you below," sounds out, fatalistic with inebriation, the hollow creak of a coffin. The air is settling, descending to the chimes of glasses falling into place.

Through sleep, through circle, wooden yawning is grumpy and hasty; the chairs ordered uniformly, beyond the front row, each one positioned to stare at a back. From the grooves that were made the previous night, the floor is now alive to a bone-bag of clanking rhetoric, scattering idealism across its surface. An ejaculation of words to "comrades, brothers, and sisters" and others is here to rouse "Us," spinning in revolutions, as the next after the next revolution being the one that will free us.

"We are going to send a message to that woman that we are a community and that we will not be beaten by policies that seek to breed divisiveness, resentment and

20

jealousy. We must say to them that we believe in the values of tolerance, compassion and social cohesion. These are the values that the Labour Party has always held dear and we don't need to change them, we just need to believe in them again." The "us" applauded him higher. "Some people in my party, the party that I love, the party I have put my trust in, seem to believe that the best way to defeat the Tories is to jettison all that has made us strong. I would say to those people: real, honest values will never be out of date, because the common good does not have a price on it. It can't be re-modelled and put into a competitive market to see if it sells. It is something we must always keep within us, because it makes us better people. If you don't have it, then go and join the Conservatives spivs and make your fortune, but don't stay and ruin my party!"

Reg Tinnion was our Labour MP. He had been in his job nearly twenty years, his employment secured like the interlocking lines of a crossword where empty spaces are filled with empty rhetoric. He would never lose his job.

Out and about, Reg Tinnion circled the town at intervals, prompted by a duty to be seen, to remain known, to service the lips with his well trained ears, to filter the noises of disenchantment as he swooped for a vote. But he was never really listening to what was being said by the preachers, never allowed himself to be caught up in a surge of ideologies that sought the oxygen of a purpose.

"Something's got to be done about the youth club, get them tearaways off the street."

"We've got to show those bosses that they need us more than we need them."

"You wanna get a message to the Labour Party that we are ready to fight."

"Most people know it's the right thing to do."

Reg had a nod for all, feeding off a sense of optimism and recycling it before sending it back, all full of billowing conviction. But he was far far away from the unscheduled preaching of day-to-day life that was living in every pocket of the community he represented. You could hear it on the buses that dropped off at idle places, spreading the nourishment of chitchat; the escapism of gossip easing the burden of the masses.

This was a time of an age's last gasp, where regular double decker buses, with numbers we all knew, transported a mushroom cloud of banter between places and spaces. Now only remembered, the anachronism of conductors, cheery-ed by tales, spinning off roles for the kids at the front, offering a presence easily taken for granted, a sense of safety and belonging, conducting a choir of fag breathing women exchanging the laundry of anecdotes. It seemed like they all knew each other, and if they didn't, then they would by the journey's end, degrees of separation faded by the sharing across seats.

The motion of turning back to engage another was something that seemed natural back then, bending frames and facing with a welcoming countenance. The motion kept the heart beating all around town. Turning in pubs, crowded by the hypnotism of sound, of utterances and paraphrases, and sweet-tinted plagiarises, second hand stories and congregating comedies. Not yet, the fear of confrontation caused by the ideology of the self, not yet the mistrust of an age soon dawning.

Things tightened for Mikey in 1984, losing his job at the pit, returning to Manic Street more frequently for food and encouragement. It was good to see him, but despite an admirable energy, his words now barked more with anger: Back to square one, back to the wall. Firing squad has profitable bullets. Use these bullets to kill those who question and use the unclaimed pay packet to fatten the boss. Squeeze the job into somebody else's time, or spread it around so nobody knows. Then save your bullets to sell, to some Central American dictator with a soul for the Yankee dollar.

Danny Madison's out on Manic Street, pushing into the wind with a red rosette on his chest, like a fish suffocating on air: "Listen to me. I am talking to the reason and conscience inside of you. This government doesn't care about working class people, or the weak in our society. It's only about winners and losers, and you've got to be selfish and ruthless to be a winner. Thatcher wants to break up society, sell the pieces off to the highest bidder. She's got a special relationship with Ronald Reagan – a criminal against humanity. This is a man whose government pays for death squads to kill innocent people in Nicaragua. Is that what this country is about now? Making friends with murderers?"

His leaflets flapped and flailed, breathlessly hooked on passers by, to discard at their leisure. They joined the smudged causes and pleas of a hundred others in a ticker tape parade of indifference, like the insubstantial betting slips crunched inwards by those signing on at the bookmakers. They count in pennies, filling the hours of inactivity with donations to chance. In the smoky net they exchange tips and predictions, distracted and sustained by banter, beyond the rush for a bet before the flummox of disappointment. They are some quaint, amateur approximation of the sharks in the stock exchange, playing games with paper money, roused at intervals to speculate. There is a chaotic connection between the inconsequential flutter for beer money and the buyers and sellers animated by profit scribbling the wills of thousands made jobless by their risks.

Somewhere amongst the cause and effect, the cold comfort of an irony linking somebody's loss with somebody's gain; an idea of society reinforced. Though they trudge from the bookies with less than they have entered, they have bought some time, and a rest from pessimism, contemplating a notion that their collective negative of bruised odds is merely because somewhere there are others with a healthy positive: A positive profit. Society's grim narrative has them as a collection of individuals, selling their souls for percentage profit, taking the scalps of communities like ours when their loss is our loss and we are community for sure. You can tell them by their dress, marking each scalping with a designer symbol on their attire.

My school bag had no fashion symbol, no super sport spot of my purchase power. It was a haversack, once used by my Dad for carrying an assortment of basic tools to sundry minor jobs. On it, I biro-carved the slogans that were meant to cool the adolescence bursting vacantly all around. The thick, coarse material meant such artwork took much more effort than the smooth quick dash of felt tip and plastic, indulged by my contemporaries whose words were run of the mill love for run of the mill heroes. I scrawled *A.L.F.*, *Meat Is Murder*, untroubled by the contradictions of an anarchist's symbol inches from the *CND* sign. Revolution upon revolution was fashioned like a roller coaster, naively understood as something potent and possible.

Peter's Records, just off the sea front, as well as ageing with dusty second hand vinyl, somehow managed to stock music that was being identified as "indie" in amongst the gluttonous glow of George Michael's teeth and other musical placebos. I took to keeping a log of the music I listened to. If I'd bought it, I could freewheel through the tracks again and again and enhance the words in a purple file earmarked with intellectual abuse. Mostly, the music for my reviews was taped from John Peel's radio show, late night enough to be noir, the reception rough enough to belong to another place; distant, vague enough to be malleable, to be imagined into aluminium blinds, rain-Pollacked windows, the migraine of a shade-less light bulb. Outside, cars and neon, horns and sirens, late night trash blowing around a theatrical subculture.

Coloured by the affectation of movies and music, I was pounding typewriter keys most nights, dipping in to alienation and rain-soaked heroism, shifting inside my skin to fit some notion of what I thought I wanted to be. Something new had appeared on the market: a disc camera, all so futuristic to my impressionable self. I'd sold a past of football cards and Dinky toys to buy one and take snapshots of scenes to study for ideas.

Turning teen – and the new sound of numbers notching my identity – I was a fever of roles and inadequate for all. Instead, an internal sculpturing found bits and pieces of souls to cut and paste and absorb, becoming something approximate to outsiders and rebels I calculated admiration for.

But this was all fiction assimilation, offering more of the spectacular and mesmerising than the real transformations being wrought by the lifelines connecting me to my hometown, to the bloodlines of Manic Street where changes were impacting upon us all. Disharmony infected some parts, disagreements itching to the surface, fermenting as options dwindled, passed on through a brick/concrete grid. But, there was always a unity of rage clanking at the iron-gate pulpits on Manic Street:

"What am I supposed to do if the pit closes?" pondered Ray Young, his son John looking up intently from his side. "I'm supposed to move away to get a job am I? I've lived here near fifty years and I'm supposed to uproot everything? How can I cut off my ties, start again, learn a new trade at my age? How can I connect with a new world now?" he contemplated, tonal lilts carrying over the circle of empathy, heads nodding as if notes were being chimed by his lamentation. "This country has come to something when it's all about scraping a bit more profit and to hell with the people."

In the chilly, freezing air a chorus of agreement murmured, judgments clouded in the exhales of fragile lives inherited from ancestors whose times were formed and mapped out from cradle to grave.

Whenever an unknown figure arrived at the pit, the sweat-beads of panic surfaced, blinking into the light, to ignite a fag and exchange rumour. Something from the outside always caused a tightening of the bond, simultaneously wounding and healing by meshing a spirit through fear. The inappropriately dressed man in shiny new hardhat arrived on a crisp, late winter morning, exhaling the ghosts of those he was about to kill, or so the watching crowd thought. But during the hours that passed, when anger and resignation fed off each other, he was not writing off lives, but making notes about a possible future.

Bill Harris was young with relief when he announced: "Findings that show the high-quality seam of silk stone coal we have been mining has another five years' life left. I'm sure I'm not alone in hoping that this can now put an end to the worry that has dogged families in our town for the past few months. This pit is the heart beat of this town. It pulses through day, through night, touching every nook and cranny, every side street and back alley. There is some link back to this place from every business and every household in this town. That's what the Tories don't understand: the connection, the sharing; the attitude that not everything is about winning and doubling your money. With the steel factory shedding jobs to sharpen profits, this pit is vital, and now, confirmed viable. I've long since given up wondering about a God, but on this occasion, I thank him."

But two weeks later, the Conservative government would seek amputation, announcing in 1984 their plans to close twenty pits around the country and lose twenty thousand jobs.

However, Marcus Bowles doesn't see it as bad news, talking blindly about changing, about "sweeping away" and "cutting loose." He's making quick money on British Telecom shares and looking to re-invest in property for some more easy money:

"We keep hearing all this anger and bitterness about change, but change is a natural thing and the Conservatives are giving people the chance to take responsibility for their own lives. What's the matter with the people round here? Do they want government to control their lives? Hell, show some initiative. Yes, get on your bike."

Bill Harris had one year to go before retirement when he got the news that they were going to cut some jobs at his pit as well as closing down completely a neighbouring pit. "Well, looks like I'll be going out with a fight. Good. It's time somebody stood up to that woman."

He calls a meeting. He is all fire in the belly, salt of the earth honesty, hands animated in gestures of emphasis, arms working from his sides to create a space in front of him, as if he were shepherding those before him into a common ground; an idealised common good: "Believe me, this isn't about just this pit, it's about other pits and communities like ours all around the country. Mark my words, this is a stand that needs to be taken or in ten years time there won't be a coal industry to speak of. We could say we're all right; we'll soak up the losses, but what about those down the road, all out of work? What happens to our fellow workers if we don't make a stand? And if we let it go, who's going to support us in a few years time when they say we now need to close your pit?"

There's a place in hell for Thatcher, I'm sure: This bloodless bitch, economically drained of feeling, with blue rinsed soul, knittering and nattering, genocidal with affected prudishness, hypocritically Victorian child becoming murderous fascist. She's got her little American heavy in Ian MacGregor, the freakin' burgered-up yank crank, some evil pawn of the Republican Party. He probably believes in God too, with all his licked-black heart. He's got to believe in God, because the Devil's got his soul and he's sucking for air.

"Agitate."

"Educate."

"Organise."

In black and white, a struggle was being deformed by a cosy condescension from somewhere unreachable, somewhere snug and middle class, in homes mocking the three bar fires where warmth would have to be measured in pence, rationed by need, compensated by the comfort of others. In the homes of these others, the chattering of an economic reason, around mock coal fires sold as 'real', chattering and regurgitating the lies that were cutting adrift the humanity of those in towns like ours, as we chattered with cold, used words for defence and to mask the vulnerability we felt.

Disparate voices, distant voices, a clashing of words bruising the body as the skull-cracking Met police invaded northern towns, twirling batons, yahooing in charges, emphasising the divide between north and south. They marked their visit on bodies, Xs in stitches and no support from those voted into opposition. The police were sweating pounds, delirious in fat-wallet overtime, fracturing bones, toppling those shedding loose change for food.

Mikey was somewhere in the crowd, retreating from a charge, one of the many who were stumbling and being trampled underfoot. When the remnants were then bludgeoned, Mikey saw his friend, Chris Atkins, trying to shield himself from a vicious beating. Mikey charged into the belly of the police officer, head down, cracking ribs. The officer went down in agony. Mikey was bewildered in a brief moment where he had time to look down at the man spitting blood, a silent roar of slow-motion realisation at the awful significance in what he had done. Then he too was being beaten, indifferent on dry earth, seeing futures as he submitted before being taken away.

A force that was changing lives was doing it in dramatic ways, dizzying those it changed. It was a civil strife that seemed to be changing everyone. Love festered, a coagulation of needful desperation, drawing those around to be closer, to be skin tight, skin vulnerable; a twisting flesh hewed, beaten black and blue. Men who got £11.75 a week from the strike fund were, after time, gleeful at the Friday fortune. They learned to live on it and value it and when it was renewed it gave them a little colour for the fight ahead. Most days, around town, pockets of desperation bulged with buyers and sellers in a crudely assembled stock exchange, pouring out years from their tattered cotton, selling the ring that commemorated a day to remember, passing around anniversaries, losing religion and honour.

Down at the social club, a ramshackle kitchen has been positioned, with Mary Young and Katherine Harris cooking up sustenance for a crowd of miners reduced by circumstance.

"Here you go, Dickie, it's a meal fit for all you princes. It's got soul and spirit and it'll kick you awake," announced Mary heartily. "We're going to win this fight because we have justice on our side. We're in this together, and together we will be as irresistible as this meal. Hiya, George, it's your favourite, vegetable soup and ham sandwiches. You're doing a good job, George, keep it up. This is a fight for all working people and we won't give up."

Joan Madden's out with Helen Lewis, driving a white van around shopkeepers, dignified as her reasoning takes flight:

"We would be grateful for any donations you can give. I know our strike has your backing because it makes sense doesn't it? All of us need the pit to stay open, because if it goes, then you know your business will be hit. Thanks, comrade," she says as she jots down a name and peels off a sticker and offers a flimsy poster to solidify support.

Joan and Helen do this every day, gathering in vegetables and tins to reach ahead of tomorrow and keep circulation flowing, feeding unquestionable passions and silencing the hungry growls of bellies. They are more than wives, more than mothers; ceaseless in their working to animate the cause their men were embroiled in. Bella Hickton organised the mechanics of bodies restless and unsure, indenting papers with ink to send to foreigners in suits, demanding their support and shaming them for their ineffectuality. Planning ahead was her particular skill, so that tumultuous tomorrows lanced the disease of hopelessness. There would always be a meal for miners being starved into submission.

Beautiful women would turn up at meetings, preaching with passions screaming from wombs:

"Margaret Thatcher makes me ashamed to be a woman," said Liz Byland. "Does she have any feeling in her body? Does she really? Has she given life and does she know the feelings of protection for a baby vulnerable and pure? I don't think so. Thatcher doesn't care. It'll never touch her that people might starve, might go without necessities she takes for granted. Her womb is poisoned and her children are devil dolls. She has no feeling, but a love of money. She hates us for caring, hates us for belonging, and hates us for fighting and believing and hoping. We support our husbands not because they are our husbands, but because they are humans, and because we have been fed and clothed upon the goodness of their work. I'm sure she can't understand why we are not meek and feeble and ready to take a pay off. Like I said, she has no feeling."

For so long, the community resisted, working as a self-contained unit and living through working class clichés. When Kevin Butcher arrived in town with his insidious promises to forge a new union once there was a return to work, we sent him packing. Financed by *The Daily Mail*, he was going around the country trying to divide and conquer, trying to stir up resentment between neighbours and families. He needed a police escort to avoid a righteous kicking.

Nevertheless, there grew an awareness of the gradual erosion of spirit and belief from the hungry bellies at soup kitchens, lined up in a tin-drum symphony of doom.

"This is the last fight," said George Lewis. "It's the last fight, and to many it looks like a pointless one at that. We've been sold down the river by the fuckin' Labour Party. Neil Kinnock would rather have a few more votes than stand shoulder to shoulder with us. Who would have thought it? Let down by people I've worked with for decades. We're swinging at the air now. Might as well give up."

An explosion in Brighton found cheers round our way. We were cut off from capital gains of loss and sympathy, more lamenting that bloody Thatcher got out of it alive. And Tebbitt's disabled wife on teary television screens only met with a crabby, choked joke to tell her to "get on her bike then."

"They're blaming the miners," said George Lewis. "Well, it's not our way, but whoever did it I can forgive, because this Tory government needs blowing to pieces. I don't care if all their goddam limbs are sent flying into the air. I have no tears for their families, who couldn't give a toss about the lives being ruined by capitalist ideologies. Go on, blow some more of them up. Go on, try again, I'll light the bloody fuse next time."

Lawrie Burnham is throwing his heart out. When it was all he needed, it was all Anna Burnham needed. They were idealised, crystallised, could never be satisfied, and they held placards that meant something sometime. Now they were cracking the air with the arguments caught down cul-de-sacs of reason. They were spilling and unravelling, drowning the girl caught below. They could not cope with the intricacies of the present, too cut adrift to see solutions beyond the final argument being anything more than the prelude to a slammed shut door. Lisa, upstairs, had no songs to play over the row, no way to find fantasy in the rhymes of the times. She's got a slide show of images of what goes on below, words struggling on the tails of her thoughts, searching for blind alleys to hide, in shadows where no words are needed and the only sounds tell a tale of love as a whore.

They were no shoulders to put her agony on, just the played out and replayed routine for people she didn't know.

Through a suffocating summer, we waited for Mikey's life to be set loose in some other direction, secretly prayed for an intervention. But in 1985 Mikey got sentenced and we were emptied, less of a family. We were clocking on, stuck in time, unable to create some tangible illusion that would alleviate the pain. We were parts of a whole seeking to heal, but we were never able to ignore the wound that had transformed the structure of our home. Every room was emptier, prosaic in its functionality, devoid of the signs that had positioned Mikey as a participant. No oil smears on surfaces, no discarded rags from buffing up a dream. No work in progress. We ate differently, cleaned differently, watched ourselves in mirrors differently, consumed by a shared regret, noted in off-angle perspectives staring at the corners of walls where spiders dallied uninhibited.

Danny Madison was back in town in 1986, intent to run as an independent candidate in forthcoming elections. His meetings echoed in the newly bloodless boarded up houses:

"I remember when these houses were all occupied; when there was a sense of belonging to something, to a community. This idea of community is something the Tories can never understand because you can't put a price on it. They want to destroy communities, happy that somebody can buy these houses up cheaply and sell at a massive profit. Don't you think the families that have been forced to leave their homes and find work miles away would like to come back? Let me tell you, if I won your vote I'd fight tooth and nail to keep the pit open, to make sure families can be brought up in this town and not have to leave. Don't think Reg Tinnion and his Labour Party care about fighting for working class people. They're too busy fighting with each other and every now and then some windbag talks a good talk but doesn't do anything."

Language rooted in a past that could no longer stretch its limbs and offer rebirth in a consensus now slowly atrophying. On blinking television screens, all the glamour of a new ideal in puffed up suits and squared off power styling. This is the amputation of history, substituted by the fake plastic movements of a mass bought by tax cutting dismemberment. There is no need to care, just to ignore and let slowly slip away. The daily rumble of this town, waking up Manic Street, grows more distant each week, lets apathy keep sleeping the voices once booming on the pulpits now vacant. An industrial rhythm, a vigorous cacophony, a chain reaction of sound and light: all have been quelled, the preachers waking too late to catch the early bird ears, their mutterings now faded in echoes and signify defeat.

"You used to be able to catch one bus, but now it takes two, and it costs twice as much and takes twice as long. Well, you just think you might as well not bother, and just stay at home instead. Hey, we've got no money to spend anyway. You say the same things, and get into the same past, and you're trapped in a round of memories you'll never get back. Well at least my generation had something once, I suppose. I'll take that to my maker, get let in for good behaviour."

"Aye, God will help us won't he," mocked a preacher of many years, all of them postcards bound by elastic bands, dust-withering in an attic. "Better save a bit of money mind. You know with this new God, you're gonna have to pay off your sins, and then invest in a plot in the clouds. Then you can charge your angels for the comforts you've taken for granted." His words were spitting fire, "No, I'll see you down below. Great God's done nothing for me."

In 1987, Bill Harris wasn't much enjoying his retirement, the aged years consumed by a sense of failure, by something inevitable and prosaic in the waking hours and clocking off days. He felt much older; saw the broken spirit in the mirror every day. He walked around the town a lot, round by the shrinking pit, along the sea front, finding a makeshift pulpit on a wall on Manic Street, exchanging small talk with the sighing neighbours losing their innocence to the gutter, drained of the kind of naivety that kept families together, a naivety made up of a willingness to live on trust and not fear that the trust would be exploited.

"Hey Bill, how's it going?" asked Ray Young, taking a seat beside Bill on the brick wall.

"Not so bad Ray. How are you?"

"Not so bad," replied Ray, using a common refrain around these parts, based on some notion of a world filled with starvation, poverty, injustice. "My boy's going in the army next month. Of course, there's some worry, but he's proud of himself and we're proud too."

"If it's a good and right cause, then he is a hero."

"You think we're gonna kick these Tories out next week?"

Bill looked to the intangible air, to "the heavens" for a prayer. "I can't see it Ray. Who's gonna defeat them? There's not enough people seems to want an alternative anyway. Something's in the blood, something like greed. But it's got a smile, got its respectability now. Killing your brother shows initiative now. There are plenty of people getting rich so the Tories will have bought enough votes I'll bet."

"Well, they can't take our spirit, eh?"

"You'd think not, but it seems everything has a price."

Bill Harris spun out the philosophy, got sidetracked by nostalgia shared with Ray Young, then went about his day, around the parts of town he knew so well, sharing his pension with the bookie, the baker, the publican, taking in the sea air and working up an appetite of contemplation. He had solitude, used it to organise thoughts, dilute disappointment and find something to look forward to.

He was not the only one with solitude. Transferred to a prison further away from home, Mikey was being asphyxiated by regret. Not for him a sense of injustice or anger, but rather a crushing feeling that he could no longer touch the dreams he had nurtured in waking hours. Now there would be no realisation of them. Instead, he had to face a future where stability was the dream, where finding some place in the world again was all he could achieve. Bars diminished his sights; his perspectives a flickering image, a mocking show reel in phoney celluloid.

On Manic Street, litter congealed, caught in the hollows of homes, the abrasions in windows. Blown in from somewhere successful were the discarded durables, which once wrapped the consumer dream, now roughed by the streets they had been corralled along, stamped like headstones and tossed into the anaemic gardens on Manic Street.

George Lewis got dirt under his nails from clearing away rubbish, ran them briefly under a cold tap before taking to the streets, clothed in the rags of enfranchisement, hand in hand with the wife whose strength he relied on. He carried his intentions like a cross, trudging to the polling booth under no illusions, placing his mark in a foreign spot as some pitiful protest, then down to a Labour Social Club whose function had become archaic.

Throughout the day, filtering in, the faces of voters who'd once shared a common ideal. Now their crosses were disparate and divided, thrown onto paper with only the slightest hope.

For Danny Madison, the hope was more emphatic:

"Things have got to change. The country is sick. If enough of us believe, we can change things. Give me a chance and I'll take it. Socialism isn't a dirty word."

Dad voted for Danny, despite the scorn of his friends still stuck in Labour: "He might not get in, probably won't in fact, but he deserves my vote more than Tinnion. At least he's got some ideas, got some fight in him. All your Labour votes are just to keep things the same. And it's all sliding to Hell. What's Tinnion gonna do? Warm us with his hot air? You make me laugh."

"You've wasted your vote. The kid doesn't stand a chance. The only way to fight back is to show we still have unity. You're doing just what Thatcher wants, helping to divide the working class. She's destroying the unions so we don't believe they can do anything. Well, you might as well have voted Tory."

"Hey, don't talk to me about working class. The working class have done it to themselves. Look around the social club. You'll find plenty of copies of *The Sun*, plenty of 'em easy prey to prejudice and greed. Plenty of cut off noses, spitting faces, spiteful spitting racism and sexism. You all want a Labour Party that'll stop the sea coming in. I'll tell you this, Reg Tinnion didn't go down the soup kitchens during the strike, didn't stop putting petrol in his Jag. Then you've got Len Murray, happily retired as TUC leader taking his place in the House of Lords with all the other rich pricks. And bloody Kinnock didn't have the balls to back Scargill. His party's after middle class votes, not working class, so don't talk to me about wasted votes."

"Aye," agreed George Lewis. "That little Hitler Rupert Murdoch, and his little Goebbels Kelvin MacKenzie are laughing at the working class who buy their filthy little newspaper. *The Sun* is just there to lie and keep people stupid. Who cares now about the thousands of people kicked out of jobs when the paper moved to Wapping? I talked to people who'd gone to Wapping to protest and were beaten up by the police. Same as they did with the miners. One bloke told me he saw people inside Wapping waving champagne glasses towards the protestors outside. *The Sun* is a propaganda rag for Thatcher, that's all. I wouldn't wipe my arse with it, 'cos it's already covered in shit."

They carried their crosses all around town, filing through community centres and schools, youth clubs and churches, futile indents offering a whispered scrawl for the Holy ghosts, thoughtless in booths, curtained like a magic trick, then in a puff of smoke possibilities are gone. We are fooled, we are mocked, and we are delivering arse-wipes for the successful and speedy. We are clogging the arteries of our town with our misplaced loyalty, choking on notions, winded by rhetoric. We cling to a past that has already been pulled from under us, 'til we fall to the ground, smashing bones, leaving cripples to contemplate. And how they do: In the ill-fitting temples of pubs and clubs, baffled by graphics swinging to the right, suspending our Time, marking the end of a history. It's all too obvious too early; not even a flicker of hope. Results are announced on the basis of a handful of declarations, and we are numbed by display, sent packing back to our places and spaces, to grow old and grumble.

Through a fitful night, the self goes culling, wreaking genocide throughout towns like ours: an ideological cleansing, where dissenters choke on the rope of laughable choice. Eyes bulging, throat tightening, squeezing the working out of class, so that down below you can slip under, find some space in the cancerous air and smudged print of prejudice, see your life through own brand lager in packs of twelve, and the fattening grease of meals served quickly. Somewhere, through bloodshot eyes, is aspiration and security, a middle class that can chatter and natter and give donations to the Money God. Make your choice; put your soul in the bank.

Sean Patrick littered the spaces where he found solitude with his anxious thoughts and awkward introspection. At fifteen, he pondered when others partied. This angst wanted meaning attached, but he could provide none, so that his words were juxtaposed symbolised clattering about his head, too abstruse for articulation to another soul. So he sought the exile of places he convinced himself only he knew of; the caves where he scrawled on rock, the abandoned, the rattling alleyways where violence lingered, and from there administered back-street catharsis: "These words can kill, is allowed to sink in. I don't want them reflected back at me. Another cheap vodka, another vomit is as far as I can travel. It feels like continued slow motion blinking. It seems to be closing in, gasping circles in wonder in exhales I can't remember. Out of breath words can't stop it. The fixation becomes clearer – she could be the love giver. Today has been the longest day; the argument that didn't stop, the blackened taunted day where the ages I have grown from had no time for sympathy as their anger betrayed lies about an idealised past. We are family no more."

Ballot papers and broken glass, were etching suicide in football pools, raining down alienation for a generation with nowhere to go. Drawing on mainlines, drawing on thick fumes from flaking rollies, and working out a score draw for the loose cash to belong. Depositing ideologies and cynicism, selfishness and consumerism, the blues are gluttonous, puking the too much into a crack in the world.

I have crossed off the school life, into college with a flourish, taking some snap shots for my friends to decipher meaning. Julianne already has my heart, by proxy and by the approximation of lovers' tales. We ride the fairground; sleep on whirling waltzers, too keen or too bored to go home. We are in the system of the artificial rhythm of a grubby fair that has come to our town each year for as long as we have been born. It's a microcosm of our town's soul; all beaten up love of goldfish dropped, flapping in muddle and trampled underfoot. Pockets chime with change, coming from within and eaten up by chance. Dodgems bump a heartbeat; kids knock cans, clanging innocence to dying saucers on wooden floors. Success and failure echo in back streets as we traipse home, a disharmony of arms connected by the cold.

Fall rain on the postcodes of my heart, not detailed on maps. Walk head first through the grainy houses striving for something larger as the life spent with rusted thrills and last years' chills seeks to imagine a different tomorrow.

We're there again for the last night of the fair, calling up lessons learned on the backs of exercise books, scratching affection into skin, leaning on our biologies under iron bridges, damp with the turmoil of separating ourselves. Somewhere under midnight's sheets, our mentality rose towards the stars. We have ridden cranky cycles through summer, through autumn and winter and spring to be here. Kicking tins through alleyways and bruising love-me love-me-nots, we are enjoying the riches as they pass on through our frames.

When Julianne and I mastered the mechanics, we were covering ground through hours when the town slept. In the front seat we fumbled, watching the tide come in, throwing out a net to the worlds lived somewhere beyond.

I am stretching to die, making the skin as tight as the flesh on her back, hitting a mainline, drooling beneath the sun, hung from a black dead sky. We stretch out and are vulnerable to burn. Hips hit with the bone of late century imprisoned passion. Bone crushes bone under shrivelled sun, sucking the juice until the sun sets to orange. She is lanterns, pricking the skies, dashing on piano colours, dripping into my mouth. The taste has us happily drowning, drifting out, and twisting in tributaries, through veins to the leaking taps on cracked ceramic. We are snapping bones in Polaroid ecstasy, shooting at lives.

Exterior to the flat image, she is defined as mother, in ceaseless motion to make ends meet, ushering her daughter Jenny into hand-me-down clothes, open to mockery in a school yard full of ills, hop-scotching on the numbers subtracting possibilities. Natalie is like her, in a spirited defence against the other have-nots whose parents balance books by some other means. They are trapped behind wire, developed and fingerprinted with an immediacy that lets both Julianne and I become a part of them.

"They seem so distant," she says of the square blurring with gloss. "They seem to be pulling away. It's beautiful in its detachment."

"Keep it, Jules, paint it for me. Make it warm with colour. Throw on affectation. Make it lie."

For close to a year, Julianne and I existed vicariously through the images we shared. I said love to her in flashes, and only occasionally got it back in brushed dashes.

Some time after the Tories won again, they laid off the last of the mine workers and began planning a demolition.

The phrase about town was that we lived in a "rough area"; that there was some inherent danger in passing through places like Manic Street. It didn't register with me, for though I knew it was no middle class paradise of flag waving, dog walking, clink-clink drinks on rocks, it was a home I didn't immediately associate with danger. But, whenever a few of us went into the town centre and mentioned our area, there was a pantomime response as if all the wickedness in the world emanated from there.

I suppose I just wasn't noticing the changes, like the ageing of the self, or the family and friends around you, or even an insidiously creeping disease of the body. What seemed most noticeable was a sense of despair, a drudgery infecting all.

The Thatcher years were all about competition, with winners and losers, self-interest and fuck the rest. Marcus Bowles had ideas for the street that had once been his playground: "You see these places, dirt cheap at the moment because it's such a shitty area. I should know. I used to live there. It won't take much to clear out the rabble that still lives here and then we buy up the property and the land and build half decent houses which can then be sold at an enormous profit."

It felt cold in 1987. Although such generalisation misses the nuances of the year, in my memory – and at the time – there felt ugliness about the year, a discomfort that seemed to dominate even the summer, when the warmth was exhausted and sunshine speckled through machines, asthmatic and tainted, unable to find glory. Sitting my final school exams, staring out of the window, the view fuzzy with failure and the spattered prose of frustration, I felt the nausea of expectation.

It was the year The Smiths split up, the year Margaret Thatcher got enough votes to win an election and the steel factory closed and the year Dad lost his job at the pit. Julianne no longer wanted to share emotions, moving away on the back of her parents' profitable shares. It was probably the end of my innocence, when the stories I was writing lost their sense of adventure and their clearly defined heroes, and scuffed knees on gravel tasted the grit of realism. From lilting lines of adolescent yearning to staccato polemics, I was happy to indulge nihilism with college outsiders: Susie Pilgrim, Paul Matteson, Adrian Bryan and Tracy Baker, their clothes as dark as their outlook. There was no longer a desire to imitate the heroes from films, but rather to wear the scars of my anger.

In truth, this creative re-birth was just a facet of something that had begun at the decade's start. The 1980s were certainly filled with glossy and superficial pop stars and by 1987 I had rejected those types for such bands as The Clash, The Smiths and Joy Division. But this was a natural development. Thatcherism had had the most profound effect on me, evident when, as a thirteen year old, I made a list of famous people who supported Thatcher, deciding they were complicit and deserved unreserved hated. I hated Paul Daniels, Steve Davis, Bob Monkhouse, the happily ignorant celebrities such as Noel Edmonds and Jeremy Beadle, gluttonous in their smugness.

What is wrong with this country? Is a tax cut such a big deal? We don't earn enough to feel any benefit from the tax cuts. But we need the health service, the schools, and the community that taxes pay for. We are being severed. We are haves and have nots, rich and poor, on the impoverished side of a divide. Them, and us, North and South, divide and dilute.

Liz Byland and Brenda Maines, dropping their daughters off at school, are united in interplay of re-heated arguments, re-told with bias, a shared disaffection with their husbands, in and out of work, lives intermittent with love.

"Her down the street's walked out. Sez she won't be going fifty miles away. I don't blame her. Mind, I dunno what we're gonna do. It'll be like a ghost town around here now the pit's closed."

Tony Perry switches the sign in his café window to *Closed*, a long yawn before the usual closing time. Sheila Perry works abrasive circles around the coffee stains from a morning procession, and then moves outside to rattle shutters over windows. Turning to look over the road, to the sea front, prosaic with dog walkers and the bored, she offers a life: "We didn't have a car when I was little, so when we got the bus to the sea front it seemed like a long and exciting journey. I didn't count the number of miles or measure time, just felt anticipation and excitement building to burst. Me sister, me cousins, mam, aunty, we'd be there on that beach for hours, excited by the water, the sandcastles, the waves, the pebbles, the picnic. Then we'd go to dad's café to help him clear up, get some fish and chips on the way home. Traditions kept us strong."

A pause lets in a sigh, deflating some romantic revisiting with:

"You get older, you mark things more. I know now it was only about five miles to the beach. We could get there in ten minutes, save some time; time scalped from the end of a life and transplanted to the present, just for breathing space. But we wheeze on time, enduring a slow suffocation of debts, squeezing the margins for diminishing returns. We measure time by profit and loss, living arbitrarily from travail to travail."

Sheila and Tony take time to the sea, their unsure footsteps towards some cold comfort memories. They moved from location to setting, from prosaic to evocative for a little while. But teens on the sands were there for retreat, were bored out of their minds. That's why they got drunk on the cheapest of alcohol, measured in litres to befit its role as catalyst to function. Kicking against the pricks:

"I'm not gonna conform. Who wants to get a dead end job and do the nine to five?" says Susie Pilgrim, dressed in black as a celebration of difference. "First chance I get I'm getting out of this shit hole town."

The group agree, each one of philosopher, theories enabled by alcohol, theories spilled out and diluted, scattershot.

Bill Harris looked on the group as he walked on the sea front. They made him apprehensive. They seemed so alien in their mass of blackness, their piercing, and their apparent nihilism. In truth, he had no need for anxiety. They were embracing disillusionment because it was something they could have and believe as their own:

"This is my nihilism," Susie remonstrated with me. "Too many people slip into a routine so early in life because they are afraid to try something different. And they stay that way for their rest of their life. It's a belief in so-called moral values, but it's really just a belief in the comfort of being separate from the other, from poverty, violence, and the unpredictability of passion. It's the value of a house, a car, the latest hi-fi or bloody dish washer. I don't believe in any of these things, don't believe in God, but I ain't going to hell 'cos I don't believe in the Devil either."

I knew that behind this disassociation there was humanity, empathy, and selflessness. Bill Harris had nothing to fear from Susie Pilgrim or the other characters hanging around the beach in their strange attire. He had more to fear from the youths conservatively dressed, who always shouted abuse at Susie and her friends:

"Fuckin' queers!"

Sometimes they spat, threw things, just to get their kicks. And they only ignored Bill Harris because in his retirement he was slipping into the crowd, retreating to numb spots, more wary now of the impossibility of lost causes. Diluted by defeated, he occasionally meandered into anonymity, a somewhat duller beacon for the many who knew his face.

"Morning, Bill."

"Morning, Ray."

"Evening, Bill."

"Evening, George."

"Good night, Bill."

"Good night, Helen."

The greetings that had always been part of a joining, blinking flashes of time being possessed and shared, were becoming more like punctuation marks. And the wide-eyed light of day and blanketed nostalgia of night were splashed into a less invigorating grey.

"I don't know this world any more," he lamented. "I've been on this Earth sixty-seven years and I think I've seen a lot, been through some hard times, and done some hard things. I've killed and I've loved. I've had children and grand children. I've fought good causes, won quite a few, enough to have some faith in humanity, anyway. What now? I feel outside this world. Where's the feel for a community, for your fellow human beings? And believe me, I'm not your cloth-cap salt of the earth old socialist. I'm not interested in clichés, keeping what's old and useless. God, the good old days weren't so good for women and minorities. But now, there's something careless about people, reckless maybe. I don't know when money became so important. I mean, it seems to have become important to those who might have once considered themselves more than content."

His head imitating a universal mannerism equating to bewilderment, albeit salted with masculine restraint, he stirred reason and anger for a conclusion:

"And there's such a lack of empathy for others, because in this society it's not just I'm all right and screw the rest, it's I'm all right but I want more and who can I screw to get it. Hell, I should shut up. I've got enough to get through the days with a few pints, take the grand kids out. Mustn't complain."

This was a mood permeating not only Manic Street, but also the body of town and working class lives mirrored across the country. We live with just a few pence, and a bit of cheap sense, passing the days with X marks the spot, crowding them on to the sky above a football snapshot. They form a black cloud of Godlessness. Or else, they are a potent symbol of a vengeful God: a careless God, ready to rain down crucifixes.

There are crosses in columns, yearning for a draw, for some equanimity, for something that offers more hope that the Xs on ballot papers. It's a hope that they gasp for something above the sea of apathy. This is not a revolution; not the cooling stitches of XXX anger. This is the mouth taped by an X, silencing dissent without a fight.

"What can you do about it?" asks George Lewis, making his way home. "At least I've got my health," was the meek articulation of a class empowered by a national health system now seeming a curious oddity amidst institutions being assessed for profit and priced out of the reach of functionality.

Walking home from some smoky pub, "mustn't complain" is grumbled and coughed, mostly by an older generation who once never had it so good. The younger ones, stuck rutting, signing on at intervals, get too drunk to grumble. Their hands are dirty with take-out grub, living for a weekend when their thriftiness can partly explode, in an alcoholic haze where slurred talk of love and God taints the purity of all kinds of faith. These are the days their parents told them about, in a smack and a clout, shaped into human designs, bruised in evolution.

The words hurt most for Lisa Burnham, huddled upstairs, unable to concentrate on the despair of her dolls, discarded with developmental arcs, her imagination truncated as anger rose and exploded beneath the floorboards. The soap story she imagined had no place in her thoughts, too consumed as she was by the broken bones of a marriage cracking the structure of her life.

"Dear diary," she began, pushing the words out loud to distract from father and mother taking strips off each other. "It seems like much more than a week since my thirteenth birthday. They must have been acting at being nice and it lasted a week.

Now they are at it again. I wish I were deaf. Every now and then, mum says, 'lower your voice, Lisa will hear,' and they go quieter for a bit, but it isn't any better really, because I can still hear words, or else the low hum seems more threatening and I just imagine the rest. And they hate each other in my imagination as well."

"I'm seeing out the years," says Bill Harris, "seeing out my time between counting up the plusses and minuses. It's the young 'uns I feel sorry for. What have they got left? This town's got nothing for them; they might as well pack up and leave. I'll be all right I suppose: Got a few stories to tell down the pub, down there by me'self one day, with the missus another. Get the bus to see the grand kids one day, then I might go to the bookies another. I spend a few days down the library, read about how good things are in the rest of the country. I get through the week. Sometimes have to sell a few things, but you can't take 'em with you so there's no great loss."

"If it wasn't for the library, I'd go crazy," Mikey told me. "I guess I never read much before except for bike manuals and magazines. There's only so much you can learn from them. Arthur Scargill said his dad reads the dictionary every day. Said your language is power. The more words you know, the more you can achieve. Think he's right. God knows, from meeting people in here and going through a few books a week, I can tell you more about humanity than I ever could before. Wish I hadn't got the chance though. You never know how your life's going to change, how your regrets can eat at you in the breathing time. I can't even feel the comfort of self-pity, 'cos when I do I think of that copper's family. It's a dead end here, Petey, and I made it for myself. Keep taking the photos brother, keep doing the writing."

Lisa Burnham's dictionary is bursting; the pages fattened by imperfect sentences and the ferocious indents of doodles; pulverising pages, infecting innocence with black and blue biro symbols of that which she could not swell into vocabulary.

"We pick the songs that take us back," said Ray Young. "Me and the lads only have the music these days. We get a bit of money, but we'd do it for free. "My boy's made me proud. You should see him in his uniform looking like something out of a film.

Whenever things get us down, we think of him, how he's got out of this place, making something of himself."

"Yeh, that's something," agrees George Lewis, wearily swinging his hips like a vexed-Elvis approximation. "The best thing about the mines was the people, seeing them everyday, having their lives cross over into your own, so that always in the disparate experiences there was a shared path. At least I've still got the gang. We're the kings of rock 'n roll y'know."

He feeds the myth down at the library, with the gang, where Jayne Atkinson works in between caring for her parents and finding chances to live a little with girlfriends. Like so many around here, her life is a routine varied by friendships and punctuated by the escapes such bonds enable.

2
<u>GENERATION TERRORISTS</u>

I did not know it at the time, but they were many like me, many as angry and as alienated as I was. The Manic Street Preachers were aged eighteen and nineteen when they formed in 1988. Of course, I didn't know about the specific moment, for I was busy trying to find some articulation in my bedroom, now more crowded with the words I wanted to steal, spending hours in beautiful confinement lost in love and anger and seething definitions. But there was already a kinship built on enduring nine years of Thatcherism and the rampant capitalism wilfully destroying communities and the notion of society. Although belonging still breathed between many of the families on Manic Street - many of who had, like my family, lost a breadwinner when the pit closed - this wasn't the same street I had played on as a child. This was a more hostile place, where adults would shout their anger, stuck in doorways, half way towards escape but unable to step out. They were now a half dozen empty houses, boarded up against vandals, yet the boards would invariably attract young destroyers reconciling any guilt with a feeling that nobody could be harmed if nobody lived there.

They were breaking things to break the boredom. Here was a new occupation to hand down to generations not reared on a work ethic. No ethics, other than the promotion of envious fists. Saturday night was not just the night for fighting. Every night was alcohol night, chip shops queues, jokes gone too far, sideways looks and winking black eyes: Kebab shop bust ups from those relishing the blood, then littering the street with the spent forces once buried underground. They got too happy in the haze of another day done living, faced the despair of being loveless and unneeded and took it out on all sorts of people who were unlike them.

The conglomerate of prejudice exists at inappropriate places, undesignated resting spots, leaving their marks at the corners of their lives, spewing inebriated reason, stumbling onto turning points, vomiting on epiphanies. They are the ordinary boys, nurtured by the freedom of no one caring, breathless with insecurity, but pumped up and blanked out. They seem to be a mass, always there to leer and yowl, to tarnish language and make niggers and Pakis and fags and dykes of all those who don't succumb to their charms or absorb their ethos.

They have no names, being interchangeable and remarkably breed-able. From families who hang out on streets around this town – some on Manic Street – jowls slop out rhetoric, their working class credentials blemished by ignorance. They think about the poor only because it's them, a compassion that's as me me me as the government they despise: "Worra about us eh? Fuckin' Pakis come and take our jobs and ah've got to feed my bloody kids on shit dole money. S'alright if yer rich isn't it? Those rich bastards don't do proper work, do they? 'Bout time someone did somet about us working class people." Ask them if they've ever voted and they'll turn on the cynicism as excuse, proclaiming apathy as a movement for change, sitting on arses, on sagging couches, crisp with junk, tanned by television rays, laughing at Jim Davidson's casual racism, passing on the leftovers of their diseased values to their children. Then they're preaching "Give 'em a clip those bloody tearaways. Or if that doesn't work, they wanna lock 'em up and throw away the key. Or put 'em in the bloody army, that'll teach 'em. They wanna bring back hanging too. We're too soft on 'em these days, that's the problem."

Closet fascists, closet Tories, they're everywhere. They've been bought with promises of tax cuts. They're full of superficial compassion until they enter the voting booth: a cubicle of selfishness.

It's a way of life. It's Marcus Bowles proclaiming "help yourself" and leaving an ellipses of insidiousness behind in the town he rarely visits these days, only returning like a vulture, seeing what scraps have been thrown up by the decline.

This town is ageing, its innocence and quaint places coloured by dread. The back alleys where gossip and aid were once exchanged are dirty and dangerous. At night, prowlers size up houses for a quick steal. Fear and locks are replacing an era of shortcuts and trust. "Help yourself," is a grimaced invite or a meek capitulation by the defeated peoples. "Come on take it. It's gonna be yours anyway."

In the summer of 1989, plans were being made to leave Manic Street. Me, Paul and Andy were each going to universities around the country, and even though we were less cohesive in our outlooks, we were regularly sharing causes and effects and weaving conversations that shaped each other delicately. Whenever we got together, there was some realignment of an old order, now aged enough to reminisce about childhood and often stupid enough to attempt reclamation with a kick about on the primitive playing field, bumpy and unmarked for a frivolous football match where the same inconsequential frustrations surfaced.

It was a different world with Susie, Ade and Tracy; our little group reduced in numbers as the outsiders moved further outside. Occasionally, faces and philosophies passed through, but they were not cast into memory. With Susie, Ade and Tracy, there was the contrivance wrought by a need to imbue meaning and analysis, and find answers to questions and then question the answers. Ade had a video recorder, so we spent our senses on cheap wine and interpreting alienation.

"We are all Travis Bickle now," said Ade as a prologue to his philosophy, gleaned from Scorsese's *Taxi Driver*. "Who fits in anymore? If you don't have the money, you don't belong. If you do have the money, you are consumed by fear of failure. You can't trust anyone because it's all dog eating dog. Religion isn't gonna help, politicians aren't gonna help. Television says nothing to me, and most music is as vacuous as the singers whoring for more money."

"Ade's thinking about the Mohawk look y'know," ribbed Susie, always wilfully out of place, eager to inject levity when pseudo-seriousness prevailed, eager to introduce cynicism when happiness went unchecked.

"Yeh, and Susie's thinking of changing the black clothes for Laura Ashley. You've got the new Madonna album, right?" countered Ade.

Rumblefish was thrust into the clanking video recorder and we were lost in searches for meaning, going out of our heads into a blind consciousness; our milieu transplanted into celluloid longing, trying to walk and talk like broken heroes. We were drunk on pretension and would only be sobered by hindsight. For now we were shooting in monochrome the ideas that offered a connection.

I've got snapshots of lives to dissect: the twilight world of the sea front where characters seem static: caught in a moment between possibility and despair. They are stranded under neon light, looking which way and every way for some epiphany in the gutters. Lawrie Burnham's digesting scraps from a bag of chips, soaking up the alcohol that has made him forget. But buildings frame him where summers used to be: the consumer gravestones where his life once flourished. His skin is aged in clouded windows, his past catching up in the loneliness of an evening. As I capture him, he is sifting through a slide show of memories, numbed by a life he would never have chosen. It is in the suffocating delirium of his recollections that he remains for minutes, punch drunk by circumstances for which he blames himself.

He dries out under the sun of a bulb choking from discoloured ceiling, reminding him of Manic Street, of a routine that he could not change.

I put captions to this still life and paste them in albums, playing with colour, as monochrome is too expensive. I am frustrated by the affectation; eager to capture something of the real lives stillborn in black and white nostalgia, which were now being collated and displayed in photos at the local museum, superficially glorifying the life of the pit.

Susie is a poetry abortionist, reckless in metres, repulsed by the contrivance of rhymes:

"It doesn't work, it has no blood. It has neither the cool perception of death nor the heated vigour of life. It's for ripping."

"I can't be your judge Susie, but the fractured images say plenty to me. Y'know, they get me thinking. They cut me loose from reality, let me drift and connect. When I've finished reading I have been somewhere else."

"What about all the photos you get rid of? It seems to me, you're doing just the same. Scorched earth is a pretty good philosophy in this town."

We stare at the pictures pinned up on a felt board, labelled *Mining History* as if anything more poignant would be a mockery. Somewhere, those who remember the town's past as more than a still open wound have been brainwashed into believing this world an anachronism, unable to offer any insight into the human condition. It does not fit in with England's dreaming of clothes padded where the soul has taken flight, of designer gear branding identity like Swastikas.

We were all well aware that this was something of a last summer, indulging poignancy in outdoor retreats, sharing booze and a few joints as we contemplated an imminent dissipation.

During August 1989, the Manic Street Preachers released their debut, *Suicide Alley*, which they self-financed. Such a venture might have found praise from Conservatives eager eating enterprise. However, this was a band aiming to be the enemy within. The song reaches back to punk, warming up riffs and cadences with little originality, but there is an ambitious defiance about this chugging song, incongruous with the music dominating the scene. And the title possesses the decadent, nihilistic Romanticism that would define much of their early work. However, the band hadn't yet entered my sphere. My view of this debut is only offered in hindsight – false hindsight, revisionist rape, narcotic nostalgia. Sweat the salt from my opinions, they mean nothing, are merely the fluff of looking back and fitting my views into some preconceived arena of viewpoints. I haven't yet joined the band's trajectory.

So, fuck me, stitch my lips, for my words are a wound of ill-conceived opinions.

I cannot wait to leave town (or so I tell my spirited, impossible self) but somehow I feel I am betraying Mikey. I won't be able to see him so often. When I went to say goodbye it was the first time I'd visited prison alone.

When you go into a prison, you are immediately shaken by a sense of unease, all clichéd notions departing. You would like to cling to those clichés from films, for some knowledge to fasten your thoughts, but most people never set foot in a prison, never feel the real. The noises are an abrasion, a constant erosion, stripping away layers of humanity, through doors to the sterility of skeletal bars and stairs, metallic echoes from a routine where the sheer mundanity is punishment, where space in every essence and marking time are there for the contemplation of failure. In itself, this is the most vicious punishment for people like Mikey. Here is where his failure confronts him most regularly.

Each time I see him, I hope that there will be some spark of the old Mikey, but even when he seems in a positive mood, his countenance bears no resemblance to the motorcycle dreamer of old. The possible has become a mirage of yearning:

"I can't wait to get on that bike, Petey. You still keeping it clean for me?"

"Course I am. Well, Dad does it sometimes."

"How is the old man? Enjoying his retirement?"

"He gets bored. He spends time traipsing off to the job centre for ill-fitting jobs and looking for things to do around the house. He's in his element when something needs fixing. Said he might go for a security guard job. Mum's doing a few more hours at Prestos, knackered all the time. "

"I bet she won't stop though."

"No. Anyway, she won't have to do anything for me next week."

"Are you excited?"

"Yeh. It'll be good to get out of the town. It won't be long before the tumbleweeds are rolling through the streets. The Powers Arcade shut last week you know?"

"Did it? Shit Mikey, that's some memories there. I asked Becky Langham out in there. She ran away, and then five minutes later sent her friend Jane Shields out to say yes. Huh. Chris got wrongly arrested in there. We were all scared to death when the pigs took him outside. Then when they let him go, we were laughing like crazy. I mean, fuckin' crying, it seemed so funny."

Mikey could still spin a few tales, although they were never imbued with enough colours to take flight and hypnotize his audience. I guess old excavations were all he had these days. Not many heartening anecdotes to relate from doing time. So he drifted, let the breeze take him away from the present, blowing around the places he haunted, the streets he'd ride around, unlooping, accelerating to the open roads out of town.

On the outside exists a whole world of unknowns; unpredictable growing; a foreign field where life is being practised, where I will go to become anew. Some of my friends will leave too and some will stay. And some distant "hiya" acquaintances will go, and some have gone.

Johnny Young is aiming a rifle, trying to blind the sleepless target. From Velcro darts to bullets, the hypnotic circle is from the same template, only there's no brightly coloured circle of increasing numbers to acknowledge he is getting closer to being an adequate killing machine. He is training to kill, playing childhood games with different toys. He'd been shot hundreds of times in his youth, practicing heroism upon the bosoms of well-trodden ground where affected death made him still. Our fingers were our first deadly weapons, and then we had the popping caps of pistols and plastic nah nah nah of machine guns. I'd shot him many times, left him dead for an agreed-upon thirty seconds.

Johnny's dad, Ray, is singing his songs to open up the world: a love song that makes love the most important thing in the world. It's for his wife, Mary, at the front table with the other band members' wives; they who have kept them strong, kept them as working men, if only by some tenuous thread.

For the week before leaving town, I took my camera around the streets and sights. I was intent to find all the places I had once connected with through the intangibility of innocence. A rotting groyne paralysed out to sea, viewed from a low angle where once we changed awkwardly into swimwear. Snapshots cut sections of the sea front shops and arcades to be stitched together on a landscape of card. This is where the pit's closure has spread like a disease, boarding-up the ice cream parlours where young 'uns used to agitate around. Whitewashed windows grave the darkness inside arcades, where bandits have been taken for not stealing enough money. Gasping down Manic Street, a long shot to the ocean, where vacant pulpits no longer stop the stream to suicide.

At the pit, a lump of twisted metal and brick shows a demolition half-done. Now it's a retreat for the junkies mining for a hit.

Shops and houses wear their wounds with wooden boards like Elastoplasts, or else they are gagging the voices from inside, the ones that used to protest with vigour, but are now possessed of an uncontrollable madness, too truthful to let into the open:

"This is a decade that'll be remembered for greed, that's all. It's all been about indulgence and ignorance, enjoying the cheap and easy, jangling with the Rattner's jewellery." The preacher talks to the wind, spitting words that are spit back with glee. "Thatcher's a bitch. I'd kill her in an instant. I'd take great pleasure from doing in her son as well. I wonder what little Mark is going to do from the millions he makes from weapon sales. He's an entrepreneur of course and we mustn't grumble. It is initiative isn't it? We shouldn't think about the dictators bombing the oppressed, but glory glory glory in money to slaughter. Hey, bring some of your money here Mark, we'll build you a bomb. But please, for your money God's sake, let's drop it on ourselves."

I left town on a bleeding train, waved off by mum and dad, clouded by thoughts of Mikey. I felt alien in the new town, abstracted and subtracted from its emptying life, felt like I should be sending a postcard back home, telling all on Manic Street that I would be raising an army for revolution, returning soon for an uprising.

But the sense of alienation did not last long. University life welcomes all the beautiful freaks. My shutters are clicking constantly, taking in to renew, moving in circles of evolution that shed my skin, shuffling to a slouching beat, getting blind by night-light and neon editing the days.

A group of us formed an ephemeral but intense togetherness, and we proceeded to spend late nights splashing and drowning between lines of literature. We read between the veins of ideas and splattered the corpuscles of ideologies and philosophies, removing the symbols of our age as tumours of variable degrees, curing meanings to mirror the culture, to invoke the culture, to tell us what we should already know. And when we got bored and covered our naked naivety, we had to revive the culture with our own words and pictures. We were insulated by pretension, for sure.

Thoughts of Manic Street most often came to me at night, at points of loneliness and contemplation. Nighttime always does this to me. It is why I seek invigoration rather than restless sleep. Regret lurks in shadows, tilts at blinds, skirts through lamp light and swirls around my conscious world. The pain of such depression is blunt, more like an intangible negative spreading from the centre of my chest, weakening muscles, so that my body is disconnected from thoughts and can offer no fight or distraction from the inward looking, gouging away at my remembered history, finding only that which devastates. It is the innocence of chasing around Manic Street, the distant beauty of furry lights counting down the darkness, viewed without contraception from my bedroom window. It is the recollection of happiness and togetherness, of a life passing by and the inevitability of dying and being nothing, then twisting that inward and seeing the big nothing I am now.

I can only whiten my flesh as I see through these moments, unable to ever inject a positive, pinching my skin for a sedative.

Back on Manic Street, life goes on, of course, of course. There are just the whimpering dust devils of the departed to remind of absent souls that were once an intrinsic part of the being.

Sean Patrick's got a bunch of spiral-bound emotions in his back pocket, not filling the pages but corroding the paper with anguish that slips off lines:

"I live on edges, so eat around my heart. I live for danger and care less for love each day. I kill with words, kill everything for you. Cry for my slaughter, cry for my sins."

Nobody's listening to this preacher. He's getting good reciprocation when breathing the reflective punches from his notepad, moving on to a new pulpit to take it some more:

"Sing for my love, a song with your orchestral tears. Chime out laments in each dewdrop. Bleed me so that I am incapable of expression. Rain down all your sorrow; corrode that which allows me to feel. Cry over every letter from my heart.

Dear love, look out to the brand new day. I am there in your garden, letters peeling from my flesh as I run to you. The words become flesh as I kiss your tired eyes. Shake your golden locks to the new day."

Sean Patrick loves too easily, wants his hurting heart to be soothed by finding someone to share his pain, inhabiting another body through vaginal re-entry. He manages something of a front at college, his disillusionment channelled to a caustic wit. And he can strike fires with others when it comes to the songs that cage him in his bedroom at night. But in-between this life, there is wandering the streets, stalking for a muse, for something of the last relationship that broke his heart (everyone of them does):

"Look around, the day rests on your body. Shed me into every tomorrow. Let me see you smile a rainbow."

He's on a bench looking out to the sea, mainlining a moment of hope in finding a beautiful image. He has some notion that this will move Julie enough to bring her back:

"You smile like the seasons and your sunlit hair glides on breezes to feel my kiss. The sun is up. The sky is blue. You are beautiful and every kiss we will share will make us grow."

And then, some memory changes Sean Patrick's mood:

"I can hear your bicycle weeping. I see your life in flashbacks. You captured me in one summer's yawn and left me to winter. The months have been lonely since. I see spring coming and hope again. I hope that all tears will be washed away, that all will be reduced to innocence again."

Heady and vaginal, he births language like purgation:

"Summer yearns in yawns, weeps in morns. I see the summer ahead, painful without your spirit. I look at your face in the mirrors of my memory. I want to touch you, to feel you weep for love again. It's a story never told, the one I dreaded over lost years. I'm telling the story of the girl I loved and lost. I am bleeding on memory's streets, drowning."

He goes home when the rain has soaked him, his clothes tightened as if moulded the body – for artefact, for copy.

"This was Sean Patrick," he says to the mirror, peeling off junk-clothed experiences which have no dimension. "R.I.P. And here's the new me, with none of that swirling rumination, getting caught up in retreats and lost in labyrinthine musings."

There in the corner of his room, remnants of another neglected meal, as if losing the weight will lose that part of his being which troubles him so.

From a bedroom window Sean chucks idea-scraps to scufflers who fidget to wear love but have not the imagination to suppress sex blushing inelegantly in their language and actions. Refused and defused love rains down in shreds, into the night to digest the evidence. Sean's got another poem in him; some more wrought gothic words, roughened by overuse, and spiked to fit the holes in his skin. "Here's another scar to prove I exist."

Too fast we went through the first academic year, looking in the creases of the *N.M.E.* for an obscure band to reflect our delirious moods, using John Peel as a background when we huddled in the philosophy of smoke circles, little knowing that it was choking imagination, idealism and revolution, distilling a coarse manifesto into the superfluity of chattering. Nonetheless, back then it was a fire of possibility. Each day was made unpredictable. I loved the fogginess of the senses somewhere before noon, waking and forcing myself into the outside world in search of a pint of milk, shuffling around a supermarket, as if transplanted into some world of exaggeration, of ironic winking; the profound busyness quite baffling. I must have been still sleeping.

There was no premeditated engagement of thought or attempt to impose some kind of artistic order on the day. But I always needed the satisfaction of an image. Sometime in the night, stepping out and into a heart beat, a bottle of cheap liquor and a torment of lights, pinpointing insidious pollution. Then outwards, towards a dilution of the senses, caught in strobe-light snapshots of freaky dancers and baggy chancers, all irresistibly drawn to a loose-fitting groove.

But, it wasn't with the myriad of influences at University that I discovered the Manic Street Preachers. It was the first summer I returned home when Susie Pilgrim introduced me, with a scribbled on tape box as a compilation of her writer's block. She was untroubled by my anarchic tales, unimpressed by my fractured learning, maintaining that her own Art would only find fruition by staying within the culture she had been dredging up and turning over all her life.

"The intellectualism of university life is a placebo for the brain. Sorry Pete, but I've got to stay here for my muse. It works y'know, because they are no distractions, so I've got to go deeper and deeper to find the soul. Anyway, listen to the Manic Street Preachers. They have a simple manifesto," she said, "it's to release one double album, change the world and split."

"It seems like as good a philosophy as I've heard in ages. Burn baby burn."

New Art Riot was a flashbulb of an idea, a catalyst to creativity whilst I spent a summer rattling about the remains of my hometown. On Manic Street, I feel almost a stranger, the gauze of cold keeping the preachers indoors to argue with themselves and tidy up the past. Our furniture is obsolete, the bathroom from another era. It feels aged, cleaned by boredom, shined up from rag and bone remnants. Most of all, this home feels different, no longer quite home. It's been scrubbed anaemic, is imbibing on creeping, curling sepia that will lock it into an inescapable longing.

New Art Riot is the faded glamour of a faded seaside town in the arse of the world. The people are spiky-rust, worn out hearts on worn out sleeves, museum pieces for a broadsheet colour supplement feature on loss. It's poignant with hindsight; full of kinship now the battle has been lost.

"Nothing much left to do but drink to a haze and dribble some words," said Susie. "We are all hospitalised here. The only new art riot we have is frosty with irony. But I will plough inward, beyond corpse-eating worms, for the only emotions that really mean anything: those still prevalent after the corrosion of a culture."

"New Art Riot sounds like painters and poets rioting. I like the idea: an imaginative revolution. Can't see where it's coming from in this town though. They've knighted the people who destroyed this town."

"We're the victims of American terrorism," said Danny Madison, preaching to Susie and I, and a collection of the disenfranchised not yet afflicted by terminal apathy. "From MacGregor to the American backed death squads in central America, the United States is a capitalist cancer wearing the shiny happy face of freedom and democracy." Danny's words, strafing left to right, shot down the red, white and blue curtain, smoking bullet holes letting through the screams of children being murdered by Yankee dollar guns. "Britain is bloody with guilt too, selling arms to countries like Indonesia, for genocide, for gutting dissenters. These countries have sufficiently robust economies to invest in education and health, but instead they want to give Thatcher some money so she can cut taxes and buy some bloody votes."

A molotov cocktail of ideas, Danny was this town's new art riot, our polemic poet, stimulating a rhythm section of agreement. If the audience weren't so down beaten they'd have got up and rioted then and there. But Danny was never going to shift the Labour Party from this town. He'd have had more success skipping to the nearby constituency where affluence could vote in a spineless opportunist as the young and moneyed Tory for the future.

Danny's pure ideals have grown skeletal without optimism, becoming more like a rage, burning and purging his humanity's tender senses. His idealism is being hooked and skewered by cutthroat cynicism, by genocidal greed, by Consumerism Designer-ism, the fascism of logo-ism. His righteous rage gasps for the reciprocation of activism, but finds only the suffocation of those swimming against the tide. Better to swallow the air pockets of interest rates, let the pores breathe in decimal points.

"Count your fat fuckin' profits," is Danny's final straw. For now, he talks about leaving the area, leaving the country, finding a good fight in a foreign land.

The sandblast summer of 1990 saw Mikey's release from prison. We were all there to meet him: my wheezing mum and restlessly 'retired' dad waiting to greet their new son, whilst I prepared for a new brother. This man was condemned to be free, wearing a sense of guilt no amount of time in prison could ameliorate. It was evidenced by the look in his eyes as he saw us, shrivelled as he scrutinized, uneasily aware of the life he'd become accustomed to, awkwardly wondering if he could be whatever was now himself.

Mother cried lumps: for things internal and external, immediate and remote, for the frayed strands of incomplete lives and severed lifelines of what we could have been. She was looking at a son transformed, drained of the innocence which still characterised Michael in his teenage years. Father too looked at him and only saw what was missing, initially leaving his wife to seek reinvigoration in an embrace. But he was keen to feel the bone bag he had wrestled and chased through youth, to offer his broad circle of protection once again. He was more restrained with me, having seen me less over the months I'd been away, but more than that, his relationship with me had changed most markedly. We were equals for the first time, and for him this was saddening because – he felt – he had lost the ability to entrance me with extravagant possibilities. We were equal too because contemplation and voracious reading had made him understand more the differences that had always existed between us. Most powerful was the sense from both of us that I now understood my brother less.

This was a general feeling throughout the summer where the weeks in my hometown were long and dull. I longed for the hectic life of University and spent most of my holidays wishing the days away with Susie Pilgrim and a few other friends who drifted back briefly.

Mikey was never comfortable being back, brutalised daily by reminders he could not escape. He spent time reinvigorating his bike, taking it out for longer rides as he nurtured to function in the new world. Absent for hours, without company, he would spend time ridding himself of the guilt of belonging, stopping at shaded spots to contemplate where a direction could be engineered. It was heartening to see that there seemed something of the old fire left when he announced he was leaving to make a fresh start down South where someone he'd met in prison had inherited a garage.

Before the summer was out he was gone and I didn't see or hear from him again until mum's funeral in December.

The groove got interrupted. The lazy, shuffling of a loose beat stuttered abruptly. My university life, gluttonous with freedom and irresponsibility, shuddered. I drank some more, cried in private, drank clichés of alcohol, made my pain affectedly public, then went home to the stitched back together family unit.

The Christmas break in 1990 had little cheer on Manic Street. Carol singers wrap on doors, give breath to the first few lines of songs, and then wrap again, desperation and belligerence conjoined in the feverish tempo of knuckles. They raise their voice so that "we wish you a merry Christmas" is like a threat. Then they rat-tat-tat-tat and kick and crack and disappear when no money is gained. It's begging in all but name.

Mikey said they used to have a Christmas meal in prison and that some of them, drunk on desperation and delusion would sing a few carols.

3
JUNK

Buying the *N.M.E.* when away at University, it seemed to be just another magazine, an icon amid a clutter of icons. When I bought it back home, it felt like I was setting myself apart, getting me back into some kind of rebellious escapism. The *N.M.E.* of 5th January 1991 called *Motown Junk* "The most scandalous rock record" of the year and cast a long scar forward, as if this music offered some chance of change. This was a need I was too naïve to articulate, death having shaken my comforting pretension to pieces.

Mikey stayed a few weeks after the funeral, returning to something of his former self to restore equilibrium to the house. He spoke of being given a chance to use spare parts to put together his own motorbike, regressed into a house of dreams for retrospective warmth:

"Get me the fastest, smartest bike on Earth eh, Petey?"

I had to work hard to stay sane, to keep back the confusion inside. I had to drink in secret, late at night, because I didn't want to disappoint Dad. Or else, I'd stay around Susie's bed-sit, or just find shelter somewhere.

Here was the new year, detonating the previous one, scattering remnants of a gluttonous culture, but still it did not want to lose the debris, which would now be poured over by talking heads in sound bite responses, colouring experience through a nostalgia for all that was crap. As wrecking balls tore apart towns such as mine, there had already begun reclamation of a past that had barely exhaled its last breath. In equal measure, the atrocity exhibition of discomfort, the frailty and pointlessness of human existence and the erosion of the senses seethed and clotted the memories of bit parts from consumer artefacts. Yesterday's must-have toys would no longer fade with the ethereality of dreams, and every event, second hand through television, would be relived and re-imagined by those desperate to be seen to have been living.

Away from home, I amputated feeling with licensed anaesthetics, got caught up in *Motown Junk* and got further away from home. Slap down another pound, slap down another dollar, slap another currency into the palm of the downtrodden. They've got a catchy tune from a life on the chain gang. They sing it with anger, sweetened with a chorus: "Motown, motown junk" rattles around the confines of tinnitus-repetition. Confectionary tunes dull the senses, keep the masses passive, aesthetic junkies mainlining, drifting into "cheap dreams" of sweet love, my baby love. Nights in clubs, taking the hits and swaying with the other junkies and their mouthing learned from jean adverts and a fucking bunny cutting up the cute and sugaring the chorus. Welcome to the wonderland of the complicit; not conscious of conscience, the wobbly-legged solipsists are at peace with a world they are free to ignore. They and I and you and we are the accidental Expressionists, coarsened by pitiful affectation, zombie-freaky-dancing undercover nihilists. We hate for sure.

When you leave the club's vibrations, you're always outside, stranded and "Numbed out in piss towns" and always alone. But it's fine because, enough junk stops your brain thinking, lost in candy-coloured images of the heroes we can never be.

You see, back on Manic Street, they can't afford those jeans, so that there's always a sense of defeat from the teens coming through, bludgeoned by commerce. We are second best in this world, but we're doubly fucked because they want us to think that we can become something else, something alien. And as we strive to touch a manufactured perfection, our souls are corroded, our perception corrupted, and we are fucked into thinking that we are better than the mass of second bests. If we hate ourselves enough, surely we'll buy their products, right?

Slapped up near the sea front is a poster for aftershave, the kind you need to speak another language to appreciate. Splash on the corrosion, let the acid burn to the bone because skeletal is the new look for a population rattling down to the job centre like loose change.

Faces are weather-beaten by rain conducted and thrashed out by ocean elaborations, and they are never able to find seductive lighting for retreat. And the women around here, they don't look at the heroes and swoon into a flirtatious dance. The mating ritual here involves junked-out nights of cold fumbling and back street fucking. Idealism aborted, past life aborted, make-believe future aborted. The salt of the Earth is a ceremony of fish and chips, working class archetypes retreating into their homes, fearful of the new breed taking the intellect out of class. They kill their kids with their ignorance and prejudice, opening vaginas like fast food polystyrene, and chip away at innocence like a slow bleeding abortion.

I am ripping myself from this narrative womb, for timeless disintegration, for hours turning into days of jump-cut dialogue, cutting up the arcs leading over the rainbow. I am angry about loss, holding back acid tears, sniffing meths, and slipping into infinite worlds that take me further and further away from tender memories.

Dad now works as picker and packer of auto parts, pounding around a cage of auto parts to meet demands.

Conversation at the social club doesn't offer anecdotes from much of the present, as if these characters are ghosts, merely vague participants in a current life. Now and then something of an old compulsion hooks in a battered philosophy.

"Don't tell me this war is about liberating Kuwait. That's a load of old crap. Bush is more interested in the region's oil. He wants to control the oil flow so a load of fat Americans can keep running their fat cars cheaply, greedily eating up the world's resources. If it's about liberation, stick a pin on the map and you'll be close to a country that could do with a bit of liberation." Bill Harris could still find a cause worth preaching about. His passion found agreement with many, but there was no organised anti-war movement in the Labour club, for all were sensitive to the fact that Ray Young's son John was involved in the conflict.

"Support the troops," chimed out repentantly at intervals. "You've got to support the troops."

Tasting salt air, blowing sand into all our lungs, across a world choking over oil, they feel all kinds of cold on Manic Street. Sandpaper on skin tries to mould the perfect body, the perfect face; a cosmetic barbarism for lives whose footprints are fading in the sand. They mock from billboards, watch over a mass degeneration into the obsolete, but still keep beckoning forth self-loathing. Some posters are slashed as if somewhere beyond the weather-beaten paper skin there are veins able to offer transfusion. They change irregularly, growing less aspirational as practicalities and failings bury bodies beneath the sand. They are entombed alive, screaming for something, wailing in foreign tongues. The Conservatives don't hear. In the sands of time where the world is a grain of sand, in the blink of an eye, adults and children are killed and forgotten, their blood blackened and hidden in the endless night of pollution.

In case you missed it, there was a war. In case you missed it, there was a daily struggle to make ends meet. There was suicide, bankruptcy, and flashes of an imagined life on television. In case you missed it, there was an electric shock of negativity and depleted Uranium shells dropped on the not-so-newsworthy communities.

"You won't hear it talked about much by politicians or the so-called free press, but the whole thing was a fuckin' lie," said Johnny Young, made a man by killing and back home to wash out the blood stains. "Don't anybody call me a hero. That's a lie too. We were fighting an American war here, just to secure the oil. I've seen Iraqi shelters – packed with women and children – bombed by idiots in planes controlled by idiots. I've seen rockets fired at cars filled with scared civilians, burning bodies at the wheel, burning whole families."

Ray Young didn't know what to make of his son; feeling detached as his outburst captivated peers at the social club. His discomfort couldn't be rationalised without leaving Ray feeling some deep betrayal. He'd postponed moral judgement during the war, so consumed was he by a draining need to think about Johnny's safe return.

He'd even made a conscious effort to suffocate what would normally have been anti-war feelings. Becoming so fearful of such thoughts, he'd created an imaginary war; one where "support the troops" became a mantra for delusion. When he'd heard his son was coming home, such elation detonated within him that Ray was susceptible to the idea of his son as a hero, returning home after righting wrongs. It was a bliss that made him Daddy and his son a boy once more, and rested in perfect symmetry. He could not equate it with the embittered man dispensing truth to a crowded table in front of him.

"And the money those weapons cost. Unbelievable! On both sides too! It's bloody ironic that the weapons used against our soldiers were sold to the Iraqis by Britain and America. What shame there is in selling arms to poor countries! Then you look at this town, desperate for investment, for some transfusion. God, the cost of one of their smart missiles could've been spent here," said Johnny with a conclusive, dispirited shrug.

Johnny spit out the army too, leaving behind its world of "opportunities" because he was so disgusted with the war. He felt closer to his hometown, as if all else beyond it constituted an outside world where deceit, greed and cruelty existed. He came home to re-fill his soul, little knowing how things had shifted since he'd been away.

He started getting ill in the spring, felt the cruelty of the season, atrophying indoors until the pulse beyond his window was another vast outside world whilst he existed beyond diagnosis.

In April I quit my course before they could thrown me off, made plans to see out my rent and complete a work of genius so that I didn't have to return home.

I snapped, I guess. I cracked. I lost cohesion. I was drunk at the wrong hours when tottering steps couldn't take the excuse of the black spaces and hoarse gauze shadows of night. I missed classes, appointments, went out of focus like acid on art, and lost my revised virginity with first names and faces. I heard *You Love Us* when I was stoned on revolution.

This is us against the world, testing limits of love and hate through the impersonal commands and defiance of "You love us" to the solidarity of "We are for real." Here was a public service announcement: a group announcing their iconoclasm with inarticulate anarchy, theirs being the Art of joker's wild with Mona Lisa burning and middle class apathy jolted by the taste of strychnine. Accepted Art is too cold for them, for there is no love in statues only brainwashing through nostalgia. Thus, "You love us like a holocaust" accepts dangerous devotion, isolated yearning from bedroom poets, from the raggle taggle of the truly disappointed whose passion keeps them comforted.

You Love Us ends like some throwback rock n' roll garbage. And back on Manic Street, all the fathers who've got too much time on their hands after being laid off are rummaging through their record collections for something to sell, spinning memories and Presley wiggles in their back rooms and attics for one last time. Needles are scratching to puncture a solid block of past, sealed in retreat of sell-by date. Broken voices from immortal times stir the soul to flavour the present with the magic dust of youthful vitality: recollections on a farewell tour, coiling up at bedtime and indulging in a romantic search for the purest human truths.

Through isolated hours, George Lewis struggles with sentimentality, swapping vinyl piles around and changing his mind, cold comforting himself with the pictures he can still imagine: "Ah well," he signs to himself. "You can't take 'em with you." He places a jukebox selection in a sturdy box, readied for the second hand record shop.

"Can't give you much George," said Peter Marks, "I've got piles of records out back I haven't got space for. Things move much more slowly now, if at all. And there's gonna be these compact discs taking over soon anyway."

George doesn't press further claims, but takes what he can, and it's a couple of meals along the way, eating his heart and soul out, queuing with the others signing on to a slow suicide.

"What's the pride in being working class?" demands another cleaned-up face from below, identity thinned through dislocation from the bantering band beneath. "We laughed as one, fought as one, but we were just digging our own graves. When you add it up, us, as working class, means nothing; just a bunch of powerless fools with nowhere to go. We were always open to this, and we'd always played along with the fuckin' Labour Party and the Unions and some empty idea of strength through unity. But, as it always is, when we were needed we could be indulged, but now we're not, well, we're all pining for those spacious graves we left behind."

The preachers on Manic Street are fired-up intermittently, but it becomes so easy for revolutionary rants to be soothed by narcotic nostalgia that they retreat to their homes to contain a desperation that cannot look into the eyes of others, cannot bear to see suicidal compliance. Sweep through this town for an atrocity exhibition; come along you spectators of suicide. Rip sections from sacred texts and graft them onto the flesh of profane reality:

"I don't fuckin' care wha' ya do, I don't want nowt to do wiv a fuckin' kid," sprayed the boy who'd given Lisa Burnham some attention, enough to help her ignore the multiple negatives of passing hours with him. She plagiarised feelings and constructed love from bits of love hearts and three-minute bursts of greasy passion, and some reassembled memories of her father before he'd up and left and taken some innocent memories with him.

Now the boy was scratching off responsibility with madness made up of curses and blame. He was storming away from Manic Street and leaving Lisa a little more hardened and a little less loving, draining from her emotions already battered by obedience to existence.

"I want to poke my eyes out, be Betty Blue, and be smothered by a lover, because death is the only thing that's true. I am ripped and pasted, raped and crucified. Seeing a world from which I am removed, I have Travis Bickle's eyes. Growing in me is the symbol of a world that hates me. Somehow I have fallen into stereotype and cliché, heading towards the single mother of a feminist wet dream. I am pitiful and raw, bleeding for real."

"We do mean what we do," Richey tells *N.M.E.* journalist, Steve Lamacq. He's stressing in order to move beyond rock n' roll cliché, because he knows the inherent phoniness of those whose lives shed skin for publicity, and who are de-cloned and photocopied, blown up and fitted to pages and posters.

The Tories know just what women like Lisa Burnham are like. They've branded such as her "spongers" and "immoral" and they like to starve them to invisibility. Lisa's a "type" so easy to beat up for *Daily Mail* blue rinses dreaming of erotic auto-asphyxiation and *Daily Express* cross-dressing vicars. She is a lifetime away from cashing a cheque for her baby, bleeding in pain and crying in the dark; just another misfit like Monroe with a real pain that needs to be kept hidden.

There is a want to be so honest it's like an exposed nerve. There are lives so much screaming out for the heart of the matter, they are oblivious to pain, their auto-surgery expelling un-beautiful lies as they cut into the ecstasies of honesty. Front page carnage comes in many forms, from the theatre of war where weapons are props and the denouement is stage managed to sterility, to the scattered rock hedonism of icons burning from within, deluded by myths. Somewhere in between, Lisa Burnham's life is typed into the oblivion of "those" as she falls between the cracks of pious clauses. Her mother is an invisible drunk, her father a destroyed history. She is on her own against the world, carefully carved off by bills and laws and measures of moneyed-meat. Thatcher's gone, but her poison is left in the system, turning to grey and turning those she has touched to dust. Manic Street laughed at her tears as she left number ten, and the inhabitants who still existed there would have had a street party, but such unity was only now seen in the connected outrage of empty-glass rants.

Tommy Madden looks through the shattered glass of his greenhouse, contemplating in circles how years could have passed bearing modest fruit without problems, then to reach a point where every week he replaced panes as a matter of routine. Questioning had shifted from outrage at the inexplicable to an inward looking "what do you expect?" Somehow it was now his fault that stones expressed boredom or even jealousy, and that he was just there; to be a prop in this perverted evolution. He stood, delineated by stitches, a colourless Picasso piece: the transparency of his situation draining him of a desire to repair. He would give up, prepare for demolition.

For some peace, some sense of progress, he would join others browsing newspapers in the library or seeking out books that reminded him of a history being carefully purged.

"Are you retraining?" asked librarian Jayne Atkinson as Ray Young got another medical book stamped.

She meant well, but her words cause Ray to contort a state of mind riddled with fear and doubt to one of nauseous light-heartedness.

"Doctor Young. I like the sound of that," was a bubble of optimism, briefly inhaled before he found a study spot where he could search for answers to the respiratory problems and headaches plaguing his son. At least there was some mocking purpose in his life again, dividing his time between care and the escape of a worn out song at the club.

When I returned home in the summer, I was a howling drunk in Susie Pilgrim's arms, but at least one who was getting sobered by poverty. Sending black and white photos of decayed beauty to the local paper and anchoring them with some last-chance lyricism, purpose and employment were drip fed to me. I found my faith in the meagre static of security, rallied by the fuck-you shrug of *Stay Beautiful* and "All broken up at seventeen" like an age I was embalmed in.

Here, one feels hope in a song that is a celebratory two fingers to the status quo, the disdain of the comfortable and the middle classes. "Jam your brain with broken heroes" is a somewhat ambiguous lyric; at once a call to arms to feed off the glorious disappointments and failures of characters from fictions. These broken heroes have at least lived a life of passion, or belief, or determined individuality. Yet, the line also sits uneasy, "Jam your brain" evoking a sense of desperation, an acknowledgement of impotence in the need to look for heroes and live vicariously through their half-imagined dreams. The subsequent line offers a little more clarity: "Love your masks and adore your failure" wants to slip into the skins and walk in the shoes of those broken heroes, wants to turn away from the self and embrace the glamorous artifice of fiction. There is an obvious contradiction with the Manic Street Preachers' overwhelming ethos of avoiding conformity, but in a sense, the call here is to pursue an ethos that sits away from the mainstream, to tread the path of unrealised ambition, of inarticulate emotion. And at least when there is some copying of an ethos, it contrasts with the detestable "culture of consumption." In the guitar licks, the missing words nonchalantly signal what's missing from "Why don't you just..." This is an insouciant fuck off to a world of instant gratification through monetary accumulation, a preference to be "a mess of eyeliner and spray paint."

"All we love is lonely wreckage" once sounded to me, when I first heard it in that skin-shedding, tinctured summer, like "All we love is lonely records," and that felt good, an affirmation of difference. For *Stay Beautiful* is, as so much of the band's early stuff is, a celebration of life on the peripherals. Here it is "Babes on the run" and a determination to avoid a life of routine: "Your school, your dole and your chequebook dreams/Your clothes, your suits and your pension schemes." "Your" is repeated to hammer home the distance between a more fulfilling if chaotic individuality and the ambitions seemingly ingrained from birth, as if life were a series of targets and domestic achievements.

"Anxiety is freedom" is the final call, the point that only through thought, through fevered analysis, can one reach a conclusion not based on markets or media manipulation.

Significantly, the b-side, *R.P. McMurphy*, takes its title from Jack Nicholson's character in Milos Forman's film, *One Flew Over The Cuckoos' Nest*. It works as a compliment to the title track's ethos of subversive ness, refusal to compromise: defiant anti-hero admiration. Hope through pain. Hope through death. A fuck you to the state for not taking our souls. On Manic Street, they talk less of revolution, and though there is no sense that the preachers can change anything, there is at least a flicker of comfort from disagreement with society's aspirations.

For weeks on end, the radio seeks to soothe with Bryan Adams warbling about undying love, the song's repetitive churning to a chorus like tortuous retching. Right Said Fred offer novelty records which everybody buys as if in some process of materialistic self-hatred. We hate them the more we hear them, but we stuff ourselves nonetheless. Time will laugh them off the stage, shit them out and somewhere in a brave new future of nostalgia will embrace them anew, simply because such brainless participation cunningly gives lives meaning.

Ray Young is often occupied with his son, so that sometimes a band of mullet-brained moustached-fools fill in, sweating the pounds they've made in the Thatcher years as they belt through covers of the songs we hate. Played out enough times, the crowd are toe tapping, happy-clapping along.

The preachers are occupied with walking, offering that it "gets them out of the house." Bill Harris walks the streets every day because "I need to see what's slowly disappearing."

I take pictures of his weathered face as he stands at the sea front. Character lines crowd the scene as he paints monochrome philosophies that require little editing:

"Hard to believe now, but for many summers that beach was once crowded. It was like a little neighbourhood transplanted onto the dreams of the sands, with the people changing awkwardly next to you being the same people you shared your mornings with down the pit. I know it's all rose-tinted, but there was a time when we were all free from fear and uncertainty, and back then you could spend a day with your imagination, with your kids, your neighbours' kids, and people from out of town. Small talk and big talk touched the world within us and the world around us and had some connection with the whole of the country. I'm an old man talking, that's all, and generations should change things, but it should be something much more gradual, more what you call organic. Round here, we've just been cut off, that's all."

Bill Harris walks on the sand when he can, marking out places from recollection, waking yesteryears and curious artefacts, finding space amongst the nasal heartbeats of treasure hunters who divine God's gifts as bottle tops. Chucked from the drunken bellies of organisms possessed by an addiction to insanity, these remnants stain the streets and alleyways of a hometown turning inwards and regurgitating caricatures. Love is exiled in shadows, searching brain-clots for inspiration, for some romantic notion to bite. Here is love's sweet sweet exile, with teens and the ageing nihilists emerging from homes where there is no life left to burn. A vast canvass of chugging guitars and the crash boom bang of a broken glass rhythm section barking through a chest infection. Love seems to have no place in the free market, subject to "state coercion" and reflective that "We don't count 'cos we hate," for the suppression of one emotion has a karmic consequence and amidst the chaos of possibilities, there is anger: "Rain down alienation/Leave this country" is repeated in defiance

In many ways, there is an embracing of this hermetic existence, this exile, although "sweet" suggests something a little too much; the intensity of adoration, of lonely souls cloistered by self-doubt seeking a reflection for their pain and tasting the sweetness of a love that may only be barely imagined, sketched out in the outlines of half-remembered songs and movie heroes. Into this world "Despair seeps" so that the unity of purpose inside, the devotion to something unattainable, means "collapse" is inevitable.

Participants are dolled-up to the eyeballs, shifting like sea currents between bars and clubs that have licks of paint as intermittent life support. The city is a living organism where love is snatched in the exile of rain-soaked back streets, choreographed upon hallucinating reflections we see in puddles of misery. Labouring between crooked concrete, an accumulation of pretences, chronicling cremations of useless causes and ways of being, seeming to oppress and numb any feeling, working through emotions to fill a void; a featureless procession of people stuck in a routine. This is us against the world again; sweet love as intense a bond as an addiction.

There is love in the home of George Lewis, leading Helen through a last waltz accompanied by the grooves from the few pieces of vinyl he still possessed, kissing her cheek, her forehead, and the wayward tears from her eyes:

"Oh sweetheart, don't despair," he whispers to sedate. "We still have our health," comes from the book of Northern clichés. "Keep dancing my dear, keep holding me tight. Our love is still here, ingrained in our beings, in every new kiss."

There is transient love in clubs where anguish is propelled, meeting in electric kisses and the embryonic passion of contact with strangers. Sometimes these characters come close to a yearning and can be sustained by a love grown true through the bedroom exile of contemplation where everyone's a poet.

In Jayne Atkinson's ear, Jackson Pollocks-saliva colours whispered words that are undying and eternal, as they were when infected souls last framed emotion:

"I've always fancied you, Jayne. I haven't read half the books I've borrowed, but I used to return them and get them out just to see you. I tried to get ones that meant something to you, so you'd get the message. Y'know, like love poems or some't. I can't believe I'm with you now. Do you want another drink?"

On weekends, participants will fly close to the sun, dancing to tunes that were written for them, playing the roles they imagined they could be in flashy pop videos and the gaudy re-fill of exotic places: somewhere foreign, somewhere sunny, like a mirage in the East.

"So I'm a hero am I?" tumbles in staggers, John Young's grace falling between stools, mixing alcohol with medical prescriptions as he finds a route to the point. "Yeh, well I don't really know what one of them is. For lots of people round here, getting through the week, surviving, that's heroic. People interviewing me for the local radio, the local television, the local news, I just don't get it. I'm a fucking idiot that's all. They sent me thousands of miles to fight some bullshit war, and what for? So some rich people could keep their oil, that's all. Fuck queen and country, I didn't do it for this country, didn't do it for freedom or justice. I saw people over there with disease, dying of starvation, living in fear. They're no better off. Hussein's still there, still killing them all. What the fuck did my friend die for? He didn't die for anything. Fuck queen and country. Fuck your flags too, waving them at me like they mean something to me. I spit on your queen, and piss on your freedom anthems. I'm gonna die for something and it ain't the flag. I saw my friend die. He was just twenty years old. No time to waste time or think about time. And those foreigners I couldn't understand, well, they were twenty as well. Some were fifteen. Thousands of them, born into love and dying for nothing."

John has no place amongst the sweating hedonists who hate his words. He picks fights he's too weak to conclude, bundled into a jail cell to sober his system, and then he repeats and repeats to wear sympathy thin. I took a photograph of him on a ruinous morning to go with a story he could not articulate, and in trying so hard he suffocated it with cynicism and dismissed it before birth. Susie Pilgrim crunched it into her hand to make it more real.

"This is John Young now. See how the white background scratches through. This is the reality gnawing away from somewhere inside him, somewhere behind the façade."

This detached philosophising sustained us through waking, Susie engaged with despair, drawing blood to use as colour in her posthumous poetry.

"All is dead," she says. "We paint mascara on our corpses. Bought up, made-up, shipped out. Mark the *N.M.E.* the second of November, this skeletal year nineteen ninety-one. Richey tells Andrew Collins, 'We distance ourselves from everybody so we can always completely hate them.' We must retreat and gouge at corpses in the mirror to find anything like love."

Round our way they'd made up eight-foot effigies of Margaret Thatcher and John Major and we laughed as they burned, sent fireworks into the sky to denote we were still living. In between the ceremonial signing on, Christmas passed without religion save for a sugar-coated Lennon ditty which begged us to imagine, filled us with hippy dippy dreams, more like deeply dippy screams.

4
<u>WHORE WE LOVE</u>

At number fifty-three Manic Street, in amongst the debris of dreams rushed out on a production line, Justin Carson finds room on his arm for one more burst. Employed and enslaved by this ritual, he is numbing the parts that welfare can't reach, clocking in by the half-light of stained sheets drawn over a broken windowpane. In a moment of manufactured lucidity, he preaches to the skin and bones of fellow cave dwellers whom he has always just met:

"Oh man, I'm fuckin' getting over the fence, running and running. It has colours I don't know. This is the top of the world. Don't look down. They're blinding me with flashes, wanna know my name. I'm famous all over the world, just for being me. I'm God y'know, ready to kill. Aw, man. I don't know what I'm here for, but it's beautiful. I'm getting higher and higher. I'm throwing money."

"Let me have some," comes from the slack-jawed begging bowl of an unclean mouth, fixed in awe by cut out words. "Jus' man, give some for your people."

"Here man, take a hit; I've got people to see. I'm shaking hands with the Queen and she's being all friendly just 'cos she wants a hit. I'm doing smack with the Queen, the Queen Mother too, and Charles is cold turkey, selling the family jewels. The smacked out royals and me are out on the balcony of the palace, waving to the people and trying not to laugh. Get my photo on the front page of the paper. Snap snap snap, my bones will crack."

Justin blinks and his eyes stay shut, fallen into a grave of fantasies as out of reach as faith in security. Outside on Manic Street, slow moving shiny silver security, slinking and slurping through an unwritten past as Marcus Bowles faces a camera:

"I was born around these parts, so I know what it's like to be poor, to have to work hard to make something of yourself. I know what it's like to struggle, to face down the fear of change. But I didn't complain, didn't wallow in misery, and didn't try to blame the state. I believe in community, in people working to make their lives better. I'm not going to judge the inhabitants of these streets by the bad apples that have stood still since the pit closed. This government have helped so many in this environment, with new developments, new opportunities; changes that people have had to accept, sometimes painfully, but eventually gratefully. You see, it's a transition, and already you can see things changing for the better for those who've made the effort. These houses will get knocked down one day, and that's sad, but memories will stay, and something better will be put in its place. You know, I hate it when people accuse me of not caring for working class people around here. How can they say that when I once ran around these streets? What I find most distasteful are the phoney socialists ranting and raving about the predicament of people in this town whilst they sit in comfortable seats and do nothing themselves."

A procession of cars passed through the street, through the town, stopping for photo opportunities outside belching new supermarkets and the town hall clock. Sirens and shrieks accompanied the next procession along Manic Street and the carefully ignored ceremony of scraping up Justin Carson's broken bones. They arrested the drugged out onlookers still caught in dreams, nailed crosses over doorways and condemned all life that had once lived there.

From now, the house would mark the spot where Justin Carson jumped from a bedroom window, and he would be defined by idle chatter as "a druggy" whilst all other experiences would be purged from history. Nobody would know his childhood hobbies, his structuring of building bricks into elaborate cities or his schoolboy dreams of architectural splendour. His mother and father were long since removed by separation, their memories suffocating under the weight of present struggles. Although a few older residents might offer, "he was such a nice boy as well," it would only be a prelude to a narrative deluge dwelling on where it all went wrong. In infamy, he would become a ghost, prowling the deserted building, woken by stones thrown by excitable kids; the central protagonist of a dare to "wake druggy Carson's ghost." As the soft slap of fleeing trainers grew older, his name faded too, until he was just a ghost, a heartless plaything less real by the year.

Strange and peculiarly warming is the way we attach one significant event to places; from public perspectives such as a haunted house to the personal odes of ice cream Saturdays at a sea front parlour. When Bennie's Ices closed down, the spot now featureless would always remain the spot where our family gathered for "a treat." Tainting this purity, punters gathered around the corner to shuffle for a deal, to "go get some Bennies" or "go get Iced." The town was filled with "used to" places and re-invented nostalgia, icons of an era scarred by the cut-price surgery of Thatcherism, now denoted by the frugal potency of a cut loose generation. Loose-fit baggies, slouched in their own ever decreasing circles to the groove of "Madchester" offered the rebellion of ironic happy Mondays through hazed-days. The *New Musical Express* lolloped through toy land to keep away adulthood, turning "no future" into an apology for apathy. For sure, it was an inviting ideology and we danced to it too, but this music scene was also still young before the corporate men with gashed-out emblems of expense found profit in recycling ad nausea. Trailing behind the celebration of indifference and the mocking empowerment of drugs, the philosophy of arrogance; a belligerent retreat into hedonistic, priapic laughter where loved-up bore fucked-up, bore fuck anything that moves. This movement had its own generation terrorists, playfully unreconstructed at first, then manufactured by executive decisions. This was not the evolution of ages, but an ephemeral explosion of the modish, laying down a marker between the old and the new. In its incoherence, it merely presented a slack-jawed two-fingers to Conservative morals, and could only perpetuate itself by eating itself and ignoring the big picture.

In this state of mind, there was no place for the connection of species, no sense of every generation's need to put things right. The delusion revolution was kicking against the pricks by accident. It dared not speak of changing the world, of the obscure Art of pain, of insight or analysis. Wearing the cloak of irony, tits were a pleasure and *The Sun* was always out to wash out the brains.

The contradictions of a band such as the Manic Street Preachers were already apparent: dated at birth by a scene decrying polemics, they coloured themselves with plagiarism and pinned back eyelids to force on the new, the "for real" lacerations of a world gone askew. They sought to cut themselves off from the mainstream, and then cut themselves off from a subculture, wearing the rags of spewing the politics that harked back to impotent decades before. That they played a gig in our town, in the crypt of the old town hall was another beautiful incongruity. From there on in, it would be marked as the "place we saw the Manics."

That dark and weary February was a mess of expectation, of living the gig so intensely beforehand that when the present came it felt like a memory. We had no album to learn or distract us with mouthed impersonation, so that the experience came truer, staying with us in hindsight when the skin of the gatefold was spread open to enter into passion, confusion and contradictions. The elegance of the front cover, a glorious gatefold vinyl sleeve, stays with me: the pink hue of the bare-chest, the crucifix pendant and a rose tattoo. This was a whorish glamour, scattered with quotes and epithets like the ten commandments of iconoclasm. Whether this was intellectual shallowness or ephemeral literariness borrowed from pop culture didn't matter. It made heroes out of all who had some notion of the soul and knowledge, and preferred edification to adulation.

The opening track, *Slash 'N Burn*, released in March 1992, is as musically basic in content as it is in title. But lyrically, it offers abstraction equal to anything in the band's cannon. Death permeates the song, murder as a duty, imploring a cultural holocaust in its referencing of companies such as McDonalds and Exxon. *Slash 'N' Burn* cleverly invokes the 'N' of Rock 'N' Roll and deliberately forces itself as a hostile Band Aid: the persona of capitalist scum seeking to annihilate all before it and cure famine by freeing the people to pursue free enterprise as a means to move from "third world to first." Here, the outsider cool of James Dean and the rock n roll ethos of live fast die young becomes "Kill to live/Kill for kicks," no longer about a reckless self but about the disdainful snuffing out of others: murder as a privatised industry where infamy offers excuse for psychotic rationale.

The world of marketing and advertising will scar this land, a Hiroshima-obliteration of all who do not conform or are not open to suggestion. It establishes a recurring theme of the album; the individual's struggle to avoid assimilation. "Madonna drinks Coke and so you do too," is schizophrenic in its take on a persona, part mocking of conformity, part the Big Brother style didactic voice of a new reason. The satirical Americanisation of the subsequent line, "Tastes real good" is juxtaposed with the dichotomy of "sweet poison," sounding like a drug euphemism and evoking a sense of addiction to not only the product but also a life led by consumerism: "That's all you need," repeats into the fade out.

The politicians didn't really bother with campaigning in our town, hiring a van and loud hailer for a tracheotomy blare out of imperatives and promises; suited-up Big Brothers bleeding into hungry hearts and minds:

"Vote Labour so we can make a difference. Together we can end thirteen years of Tory misrule." It echoed down Manic Street, then out to the sea, turning corners, changing direction, stopping for photographs, stopping for a furtive fag, and then reiterating rhetoric. "It is time to heal, to make a difference, to bring the community together."

It's a gluttony of placebos in tinny barks, and in the tumour of our despair there is faint hope again.

"I sense a change. People don't trust this government anymore. Even those who made their money under Thatcher have had enough," said a preacher.

"Vote Conservative for a government you can trust. The Labour Party has no answers except tax tax tax." Words as nails come like ideological crucifixion, or whatever it takes to sell us the product. Here is the party that will get you a job to make your palms bleed, and then lose your earnings through the gashes of ceremonial mutilation. "Vote for choice, vote for change, vote for the status quo. Vote for money back guarantees." In the extended family of materialism, fear has a purpose: love is displaced and comfort is in tearing open packaging, nurturing greed and jealousy. Ballot papers are scored like love-struck flower-pluckers disembowelling with an incantation of "have, have not, have, have not." Deluded by choice, votes are cast through consciences anchored by price tags.

All around the town, the illusion was irresistible, prompting the preachers on Manic Street to sweep their paths, tend their gardens and clear their throats:

"You can't help but sense a change is coming," said Bill Harris. "I have little time for this Labour Party, but at least they are singing from a different song sheet. And the country is sick of mismanagement, of the gap between rich and poor, of the obscene belief that community is dead. Who's going to vote for Major? We can all see he offers only a bleak continuation of Thatcherism. Can anybody really vote for a man with no control, no new ideas?"

Danny Madison, once more standing as an independent, is imbued with this optimism, readily cleansed of the disappointment of 1987 by the urgency of hope. "Getting this government out is all that matters at the moment. I could take losing here if they get voted out, then at least we'd have a government who'd listen to our discontent." A friend of his had hooked up some speakers on an ice cream van, driving Danny's sweet campaign around and mixing his ideology with the tinny instrumentals of childhood tunes.

The shelf-life of this optimism had expired by midnight when counting across the country piled up crosses like football pools failures caught in an endless cycle of immediate greed. Hope was not in rebuilding through unity and inclusion, but in the quick fix money rush of fantasies of success; fantasies that were all about individuals breaking away from the pack, crossing divides by having the financial clout to pay for your escape.

"Where do we go from here?" Danny asked as a malevolence of light peeked through dreams bred in darkness. "What is this dawn bringing, but a realisation that our death sentence is certain? What does this result say about the human spirit, about compassion and reason? What does it say about the country?"

This is a vote for *Nat West-Barclays-Midlands-Lloyds*, each one an atrocious symbol of our culture's domination by capitalism. From the Jarrow march to the march to withdraw, to deposit, to find interest in accumulation, hoards marching in unison, the "sick routine" leading us to our death, to a "black horse apocalypse." Our smiles are fixed beneath the mask of consumer delirium where the superficial is some form of mass cultural anaesthetic: "Death sanitised through credit." Capitalism is a false economy, all its evils sanitised by some instinct for money and the smiling plastered on face of commercialism. Against the hard sell of "The more you own, the more you are" is a sense that such desires only lead to loneliness; vacant rooms cramped with material possessions; all shiny surface and no feeling. Around town, the billboards urging to vote are pasted with Pol Pot selling satellite television as pain relief. Each one advertises a cultural holocaust to make us forget the hope we had before the election, as if now we start again from Year Zero, offering the next generation no alternative to a life as happy consumers.

"From this moment on we are *Born To End*," preaches Susie in the days that follow, repeating the track until the batteries fade and howl under the weight of waves outside our cave. "The country has voted for CHANCE, for big bold stabs at materialism, for the stripping of difference and an end to evolution. So we'll plunder resources until they are gone, and we'll starve third worlds by lending our banks money. We must squeeze into stereotypes and act through preconceptions, and be all it is our place to be."

Susie loads the machine with supermarket-stolen batteries and we go around again, listening to the sloganeering and regurgitating of influences. Our cave wears Art on its walls, wears the make-up of slogans and iconography, borrowed and broken down to find originality.

"I'm getting out of this town, getting out of this country," she announces. "I can't live this wasting away."

The inevitability of the narrative suggests the kind of conformism that the 'generation terrorists' are seeking to kick against, as if humanity is caught in a cycle of decay, one where pessimism offers cold comfort, where innocence is tarnished from day one: "Born to end." The apocalyptic mood of the first two songs on the album continues here: "H-bomb the only thing that will bring a freedom to life." Contradictions abound: a sense that mass murder somehow cleanses, but an emotive poignancy that it is necessary. And it is necessary, for yet again we have commercialism run amuck with "McDonalds and Levi's" offering lifestyle choices that aren't really choices. They are merely saying buy this or be a nobody, be dead. It's an insidious offering of perfect bodies, beautifully radiant faces and all clicking into place with the right choice of clothes. Thus "images linger like repression," denounces those television adverts – visual ejaculation sound tracked by Motown junk – that suggest love and harmony and an all-pervading cool.

Pummelling polemics offer a brand of non-conformity. It's free. It's a choice. It's a chance not to live by fear. It's too free to be a success. It's an unmarked grave, some time before Gap got into killing off non-people.

We when close our eyes and wander through aisles at all the things we want but cannot afford, we are being transported to the "Concentration camps of our dreams," ignorant of the fate that waits. We feel cleansed in the new clothes, but we have sold our souls, caught up in disappointments from now until the next range, and the next range, always trying to keep up and adjust our personalities to fit the clothes, to be somebody else. But the faces that ignore us each day tell a different tale; that nothing's changed. "Beg for mercy/Pray for war."

"England is an ugly place," says Susie, "I have run dry of words. My cousin over in Australia says I should go over there. I think it's time."

"No way Susie," said someone. "You, on a beach? Having barbecues and surfing?"

"Yeh, that's me, hanging ten with a biro and a notebook. No, I'm going to go, leave all this beautiful garbage behind."

"Y'know, I hate to admit it, but I couldn't separate myself from this sordid pessimism. How can you advocate a revolution when you are subdued by comfort?"

"Well, you let me know when the revolution is going to start and I'll get the first plane back."

For the weeks before she departed, we had no Art to clash, but instead sunk soft kisses to remember each other by. There was never a signifier of love, never a declaration of its existence, and we gamely held off tears that would have made us celluloid in a flash. However, a maelstrom of emotions released the usual proclamations of staying on touch.

Lurching into summer, the longer nights brought postcard images to imaginations itinerant about town, re-engaging in traditions that consumed time and had remained remarkably free from market forces. The preachers set up deck chairs at the front of their houses, sipped from tin cans and indulged in the present-breathing. Jenny Byland and Natalie Maines run tag around the wreckage of cars waiting for repair, remaining in the sight of gossip threading together the lives strung out to dry. Someone next door has departed for another life and a younger wife, leaving behind work-in-progress as posthumous art.

"She doesn't need him anyway. What's he bloody done for her, 'cept drag the family down?" said Mrs Maines, preaching about morals and values, which were only half-constructed, held back as she is by the grace of God's glue keeping her own family's disintegration inside four walls. "I've told her, I'll help out when I can, and she's got Jessie as well, so she can get done crying pretty damn soon." She applies the gritty sun tan lotion to her legs, leaning forward to cast a view to a few houses down. "Look at that poor bugger. It's a bloody shame."

John Young's coughing beneath a cap, listening to his father's soothing words matching his retreat from independence to memories of "D'ye remember when we used to..." tapering off at the point where experiences disappeared over the horizon, growing too weak to sustain an imagination breathless with the weakness of need.

"Fought for his country and his government," said Mrs Byland, "and then ignored and neglected. It's a bloody shame. At least he's got his family."

Ray Young draws out the rhythms and rhymes of songs from the broken jukebox of his life, finding lyrical fantasies where everything will be alright, seeking to unite the souls of generations through the melodies of euphemism played over the run-off grooves of his son's breathing. There is peace in this narcotic-pop inducing reverie and sleep.

"Hey Ray, how's it going?" asks my father.

"This nice weather helps, Eddie. It's good to get out, have people stop by. The lawyer says we've a good chance of getting some compensation, but y'know, he's been saying that for months. But, we'll see. I hear Michael's coming up soon. How's he doing?"

"He's doing okay. He's been building his own bike, says he's gonna ride up here on it."

"Is he coming back for good then?"

"Nah. And he doesn't want to. There's nothing for him here, I've told him that."

"Ah, you're right Eddie. It's a proper ghost town these days. People like you and me, we'll be the last bones standing. You'll have a bunch of bloody skeletons going to the club, rattling on about the old days."

Laughter echoed down the street amid the skin-punctures of kids calling on youth to rise anew for one more game of football, one more skip on chalk-dust.

Many were excited about Mikey's return. His friends had heard about his motorbike, embellishing the achievement as they clanked and tinkered on driveways. There was still a group of them, scattered around town, all once hardening palms in the old industries, who continued to find thrills in weekend rides. On Sundays there were still two or three bikes outside houses on Manic Street, being toyed with like props amid talk of formations, laughter at love and sex, dwelling coolly yet longingly on the women whose arms held onto them when the men weren't around. Tools clanked on concrete as they set the world to rights, bemoaned the bosses and prepared for one more journey before getting back to weekly routines prosaic with job searching or menial employment in shops and supermarkets.

There was excitement too amongst my crowd of would-be revolutionaries and nihilists, or whatever –ist or –ism we had badged from the literary or rock movement that had most recently sparked our passion.

"...Can't way to see your brother, Pete. Do you think he'll stay? He's got so much respect for what he's done. He'll shake things up, I bet."

Several times, we had expected his arrival and congregated in anticipation, placing faith in an idea of our own haphazard creation. But several times, Mikey cancelled, saying his bike was not yet ready. When my friends talked about Mikey, their image did not equate with what I knew. He had never got over his time in prison. He'd never felt anything but remorse for killing a man. I knew he wasn't going to arrive with some kind of revisionist history where he was a martyr for a greater cause. He wanted to forget all that had happened, and if he did ever open up about it, the regret quickly smothered his articulation and sent him into a deep depression. Truth be told, he'd taken the dream he had of making his own bike and poured all his energy into it; no longer involved in an ecstatic pursuit, but rather a burning penitence where the end product would give his life some meaning. It was always probable that Mikey would return without announcement.

He came with the evening sun melting away behind him, with dusk stirred up by the revolutions of his wheels; the poetry of his motion eschewing flaming ego and priapic outsiderism. He was Albert Camus with a touch of Godard, soaked in the oncoming drizzle of noir, passing flashes of "neon signs" for an atmosphere of tawdriness drawn from inverted nostalgia. "Streets" are open to a rain of half-snatched ideas and possibilities: "Culture sucks down words" so that we become nothing against philosophers, our emptiness necessitating the feeding of smiles. Into this numbness comes a fallen hero; the self that so mocks, so that we are schizophrenic with choices, unable to choose, unable to avoid "living out a lie."

He immediately feels the sense of decayed machines, guitars whirring around the rain-soaked streets and alleyways of a forgotten town. Tumbling along the gutters, bits of words from fragments of ideas birthed in moments of agony, be it love or hate, for the self and from the self. Wearing the mask of superficial smiles – "feed yourself smiles" – sounds like forcing to fit in, or at least not give away the pain threatening to burst. "Life sold cheaply" is subdued by omnipresent consumerism, the narrative seemingly set in a decaying town that has seen better days, the neon no longer glamorous and energetic but a harsh illuminator of loneliness. This town has been emptied, its community destroyed by the ravages of capitalism, by this (sarcastically delivered) "wonderful world of purchase power." The symbolism of "Just like lungs sucking on air" evokes a sense of a town gasping for life, of individuals cast into the margins, the refrain of the title merely a means to create a mood, the words only literal in flashes of dreams where the biker disappears beyond neon lights and into shadows, leaving an enigma for teenage kicks.

"What are you rebelling against, Mikey?"

"Your expectation," he replies, "and all the other stuff that's counterfeit," then rides on to find the home he once knew.

Our home had embraces that night, perhaps the only one with emotion on Manic Street. We are sealed in, entombed within the tongue-tied fumbling of soul exploration, regressing to a source to re-fill the gaps we had left in states of doubt and dependency. An examination of worth and an affirmation of survival gave Michael's tearful words the corrosive honesty of someone who has learned to speak in broader pictures after tragedy has mocked the ego and squared off and speared the selfishness we all tumble and dance around.

He tells us he's just passing through and that nothing can change his mind. Dad doesn't want to change his mind anyway, and although I have sadness about it I am able to realise that it is sadness for me rather than Mikey. His best interests are to stay away. And anyway, Mikey's more Michael now, one with innocence snatched – or even drained, as his angular features attest – much less a hero, whilst at the same time poignantly enigmatic. I am older and lessened by vision erosion, and much less in need of a hero.

So he's just passing through, like all the other ghosts outside, affecting in the shadows the lives played out in homes along Manic Street, around town, drifting to the city. Here we stand, punch drunk on anger, using hate in insular circles, deformed in our little bubble republic of uncertainty. We are imbued with spirits already, plagiarising chip shop rhetoric to convince why we are downfallen and idle. Whatever machinations are going on, somewhere beyond reason, function to make us impotent, vulnerable to firecracker reaction and gut-thumping hypocrisy. Street brutals tell their neighbours it's the immigrants, whilst a few of the preachers on Manic Street form cohesive points for the winds to take away: the system, the injustice, the democratic process, some dust of ideals suffocating under nails hanging on. Blackened fingers show the prints of birth, lick-spitting together a womb for escape, sucking on the warped optimism of gauze-breathing comfort. Flies buzz torment into the solitude, accentuated by the displaced clarity of intoxication.

"Drugs come out of boredom baby," gives a shrugged reason for this state of mind, like they are all Lenny Bruce articulators of hypocrisy, like this is some kind of rage against the state. The needle chill gives them an investment in glamour, becoming cool-as-ice poster boys and girls for AIDS awareness campaigns where governments wash their hands on iceberg metaphors after horses have bolted. In corporate slums, the cracking icicles of dropping pennies chime the glorious resurrection of money grudgingly spent, falling into the chasm of cause and effect.

Some drugs are bad, some drugs are great; some drugs will get you into work and never be late. Whilst wars kill the innocent and poverty eats away at the poor, AIDS wins an Oscar as death knocks at the door. Sucking life from houses around this diminished town, looting from the shooting up, leaving by the back door, streets become marked by absence, existing merely on the anecdotal interplay of third person recollection.

These voices are awkward, hesitant, gagging on the regurgitation of archetypes and stereotypes, unravelling but barely touching lives spiralling out of control. A desperate audition, seeking to empathise, creates the artifice of "They need your innocence" from a male voice complicit in the exploitation of "beauty and virginity used like toys." She is weary, with a sexual passivity that implicates all who have time to listen to this wretched preacher, her state of mind chaotic. "Used, used, used by men," she cries out, in vain, without reciprocation or sympathy.

The male voice then appears equally as resigned, although beneath the surface of sympathy there is the persona of the men she serves; "Your pretty face offends/Because it's something real that I can't touch."

The preacher's voice returns. The yearning and clawing is more intense and more desperate. There's something of the Norma Desmond character from *Sunset Boulevard* about her and her "faded films." She is controlled by those who want to keep her figure slim, put her on diets, all for the pleasure of men. She is the baby doll, corrupted by those wanting to sell her innocence; those vermin whose heads are empty of compassion, too filled with the immediacy of pleasure.

Her audience can only return with equal pessimism: "We are the useless sluts that they mould," returning to the idea of control, of image and superficiality.

Lisa Burnham four doors down was a different person twelve months ago. "I was going to go to College to do Drama. Then me boyfriend fucked off saying he didn't want anything to do with the baby. Never mind, Anthony was all I needed. Then a new fella, John, said he loved me. But we had no money. John, well, he had lots a big ideas, said he'd heard that we could get money for reader's wives photos, so I did it after a half bottle of vodka. I looked good then. No cracks. We enjoyed that extra cash, so when the magazine phoned up for some proper shots, I couldn't turn down the money. Course, I didn't think it'd be permanent, thought I'd save up enough to get myself into College. We got a video camera mind you and I got on cable TV a few times. Never realised John hated me so much. But, see, he liked the money so the best way he could hurt me was by fucking around, but never quite leaving me. Anyway, when he found someone else, he left me with bills to pay, left me for dead.

So, I part my legs, push together my tits, and form big Os for the pleasure of eating tomorrow. It's a laugh to be as durable as plastic, bending my limbs to fit into snapshots: in squares and rectangles, in peephole Os. My body is saying come and get me, come and use me, come all over me. Let me be your plastic doll. Innocence has been ripped from me, lies screaming a headache into a contrived relative's head. I can cover up the cracks with more make-up in the land of make believe.

I am snapped into four even squares, stripped of logic, snapped by a cackle-handed aficionado of semi-detached lust. Transparency is coloured in by developments in dark rooms, where a skinned up body hides fractures of being taken by the force of longing. They call it having your photo taken: Taking your image. Taking. This is not reciprocal. This is submissive. Control is taken from me, gouging out sensation as cheap booze dulls the senses. I say to myself – sometimes in comfort, sometimes in despair – 'Lisa Burnham is slowly leaving'."

It's all about departures now, for the South, for a life, for the grave. John Young made it passed Christmas and remembered the toy guns he once unwrapped in harmony with his undiluted imagination. Bursting outdoors to "na-na-na-na-nar-nar" machine gun dead his friends and neighbours. A moment like sleep sits out the excitement of the kill, but cannot wait to lift up the corpse and carrying on anew. These are the resurrections, killing without sin, making giant evolutionary leaps but still killing with the purity of a bullet, a bomb, a missile or a grenade. This is pure death, but the images that stayed with John Young were the pathetic, crude deaths from being buried alive, being burnt from within, heat clawing at flesh and choking dignity and valour. And when he hated his country and looked in the mirror he saw a life wasting away, deliberately loitering as if to batter a conscience caught amongst various forms of self-loathing.

Departures occur with the functionality of breathing, exhalations wheezed out through the filthy air kicked up from the very streets where breathing began. Someone once known is fading from scenes, picking up frayed threads, bits of nerve ends for new lives already half over. Another is disappearing inside himself, inside junk worlds where histories can be slashed and burned, circumventing the mindless count down to retirement:

"I got my pension right now, in sniffs and grunts, in scratchy lighter sparks. I suck suck the big I am. I was Simon Brown with flexible tendons, reaching out in triumphant childhood when the nerves were steady, laying my fingerprints on doors flung open. I once touched sand and made battle-ready homes no one could enter, except for the characters in my head who could work their way into the fragile domain. Carpals moulded corporals to patrol the disintegration: attacked from the breeze, from the sea and from the foot-stomping predictability of elders. For a pocket of infinity, I could renew and re-mould, use manufactured plastic to re-birth citadels and tap signals from my thoughts. In open spaces we played these pretty games and made no provision for the life ahead. Touching stones to throw to the ocean, in the gorgeous plop we were emboldened by a force of nature. I touched earth, touched water, controlled the trickle through moats, felt the sun and the rain and ignored all I didn't create. Stepping on stones, across rivers and over hours and days and weeks and evolutionary epiphanies, I must have slipped at one point, must have lost consciousness, must have had a team of statisticians come in and put toll booths on destiny whilst I slept. A past was taken from me, so I had to choose something safer than suicide. I chose life, of a kind, cutting from the chase to early retirement. I am the wreckage of Simon Brown, pretty in my wasted state. I could be the poster boy for a warning or a fashion or even a trendy new plague."

In solitude, Si Brown rocks on the spot, rolls over at points when he is detached from reality. In the late winter snowfall he is rocking and rolling for warmth, condemned to this life through a choice between a rock and a stone floor roll. He has such freedom, but his world is a shell, a claustrophobic routine he is condemned to pretend in. His is not the corpse freezing through natural causes, but he passes it twice as he trawls through the day. It's picked up eventually, thawed out in newsprint somewhere inside warm press. It's one of the others, one of the faces he'd seen scoring at some den on Manic Street. It's nobody to remember, no effort to forget, just a departing character not even written in stone or offered service or flowers. It's a number, a percentage, a digit of those hooked on condemnation. An ocean wave passes over and the numbers start turning again.

5
SCREAM TO A SIGH

Ray Young sings in the kitchen, rebounds sweet soul music from utensils, ambles around the rooms for an audience he can touch. Mary listens intently, smiles in circles to understand and connect, following his music from room to room. His journey is slow, each step's inevitability removing the percussion and rhythm until he is acapella crying in John's preserved room. He cannot adjust or make new the world that has made him, so he sits on a well-made bed and taps out tears.

Mary has a palm to rest on his back, motioning in circles to retrieve the man that she loved. Inside is a hurt that will not desist, forever unconditionally attached to the boy he held like the structure of his own body, keeping him together through bonds of need and experience.

"He's not ready yet," Mary tells Helen Lewis at angles opposite to the home where memories now destroy. "I'm sure he'll get back with the boys when he's ready."

Plain and prosaic, her words have none of the excitement of the usual Manic Street gossip. Hers is a tale sadly passed on, not feeding on knowing, but eating up empathy, later told at a dinner table:

"Mary said he just sits in John's room, crying for hours. He's in a bad way, George. Don't play without him. Make sure he's at least got that."

"We'll never play without Ray, that's a certainty. The club will wait, I'm sure."

Ray's grief is in every room in his house, but it dominates where he most often sits and contemplates the life he is tenuously holding onto. There he casts out wide nets of thoughts from the worlds he has touched on, feels the sense of endorphins all fucked up and broken. Even the pleasures of passion in lightning strikes across country find a vein back to the hurt of home's skeletal room. It touches homes all along Manic Street, as if his pitiful tones seep into the lives of others. George Lewis fidgets with old records for an answer, unable to get to grips with anaemic compact disc reissues. The revolutions are constantly interrupted for some vinyl moment that will answer, but he too returns to the boy called John Young. He held him too, raised him up by hands to race to the ocean. The loss is profound. Across structure and flesh, the vertebral process slows and creaks. Across rooftops it reaches Pete Thornby, clicking biros on mocking pad for thoughts, lyrics and narratives that will not come. From shoulder to elbow to flicking palm and fingers, the beat is staccato, always interrupted by addictive sympathy leading back to the mantelpiece displaying his own children smiling in pose. Dickie Chadwick's kids too are there on hangers, marking time spent in idylls, frozen in images that should never fade.

It is still more than this, stretching out along the street to homes that knew the face before and after, to the interlocking lives and bonds that will not break. Dad feels it too, and when we talk we are conscious of Mikey, of a loss that is tangible and possible, of the mother and wife we daily miss. In our little lives on Manic Street, there are many crossroads and tumultuous turning points, but none is more powerful than when felt vicariously from another. For in it, we are whole again, touched by being spared, but equally locked into imitating at a distance the weakening sense of life, synovial fluid leaking in to make us symmetrically brittle.

I am often alone in my room, reassured by the intermittent thuds of Dad moving about somewhere in the body of the house. I try to write something to hook onto the pictures I produce. These are words shook loose on a page, the pen scribbling over the edge, scratching symbols into wood, all depth lost amid the fragile mental state of love and devotion. Poetry becomes graffiti as the poet slips and slides from despair to where? That the question remains unanswered makes impossible any kind of catharsis. The words go around inside the head, rusting in the subconscious: "There's nothing nice in my head/The adult world took it all away." This is clinging to innocence in a whirlpool of existentialist mundanity. The overwhelming answer is that we are nothing and will always be nothing, and adults ignore this by passing "each other as if they're drugged." Once more we seem locked into a routine, and though we keep asking ourselves where we can go next, where the epiphany might be, we can only ever slide from despair to despair, to...where?

The town's library became something of a sanctuary for those without work and with time and intellect to burn. Bill Harris went in there to read several newspapers for free.

"You've got to read them all, Pete," he said to me. "Got to read the rags to know what the enemy is thinking. If the mood of the country is written out in the columns of *The Sun*, you've got to know what you are fighting, right?"

"It's a good idea Bill, but I don't know what we've got left to fight with."

"Well, if you're still able to think for yourself, you've got something. You know, the people who want you to give up, switch off and buy whatever thing they're flogging these days, well, apathy is as good as it gets for them."

"I'm trying to put this book of photographs together: a collection of pictures and words that show what the Tories have done to towns like this. But, I can't see how it will ever get published so that it can do what it is intended to do, which is inform people. You know, I'd make more money taking snaps of tits."

"Ah, but you're not going to do that. I know that. You've still got your own thoughts. Carry on Pete, don't give up. If one person is informed, that's enough. You've got a purpose, and that's more than most people around here. If broken thoughts run through empty minds, they should try even harder to keep those thoughts."

"You're a poet, Bill, that's for sure. You're an inspiration. Thanks."

Bill got back in to his tabloid, a feverish index finger mentally fixing on a pen for an unclosed, angry circle or a vehement underline. I sensed thoughts ticking over and not losing anything of importance and no chance of cobwebs being allowed to form elaborate, gossamer traps.

I took an eclectic collection to the counter; of poetry and prose, fiction and fact. Dusty tracts and fading polemic, slumbering artistry and dog-eared imagery, all jostled in a tippling pile onto the desk. Jayne Atkinson, uncorked blonde with a mouth full of inescapable smile, passed flirtatious comment on the collection:

"I often try to match the books to the person, but yours have me baffled. What are you planning, then?"

"To keep my mind busy. What do you make of it?"

"Some kind of revolution where poets run the country and the Beats are taught in schools."

"Sounds like a great idea to me."

"Are you going to give more money to libraries when you're Prime Minister?"

"Only those who raise the flag of the revolution."

"I'll get mine hoisted tomorrow. What colour is it? Red, I suppose?"

"It's not blue."

"Good. Only tea towels should be blue."

Laughter disturbed the silence and clichés, but coming into a huddle were some other ones: for a vague and intense part of summer I was to share love with Jayne Atkinson, who had lived in the town all her life and maybe passed through mine in the one consciousness we all share.

About the English summer of 1993, *Gold Against The Soul* arrived and was as uneven as the first album. In typical band fashion though, it was an album against the grain of the times. With an incipient Britpop trend, this had more in common with the grunge scene in America. And yet, it is bold and occasionally self-consciously poppy. Jayne had it first and I broke the law to tape: One of the many lawbreakers in this town. Lifting lead, twisting cable to snap, chewing off copper with juvenile hacksaws, insolvency promoted some perverted Thatcherite vision of self-help amongst the population. Mrs Maines scrubbed floors for cash-in-hand to top up benefits that did not benefit such an extravagant nomenclature. Her smooth hands turned coarse, her knees roughened from assuming a position she seemed always meant to contort. She no longer had space for sensitivity in her fingers, or indeed motherly need now that Natalie had moved away from hopscotch fancies on Manic Street's pavements. Concrete corpuscles responded to trudgery and drudgery, pounding around in circles, feet squeezing dead fags, marking spots of waiting and fidgeting and the hasty, rudimentary pleasures so dear to the poor. Ways to make money keep all on their toes. Pocket money does not rattle, for that buys so little, but waits in the creases of linings to accumulate the odour interest of intangible purchase power. A bottle of cheap wine will kill more time.

Time is up for sale too. Well, it's all that most people around here have to sell: from icons of the past to cheap imitations of fashion. Moments under the sun have no second hand amusement, but are moved on at a fraction of the price, distilled of the solace they once brought.

Bill Harris opens up the velvet lined box where he keeps his medals and takes in the locked air of ageing metal aroma, its distinct smell as identifiable as on all the previous occasions he has unlocked the past. He thinks of Natalie Maines as a child in Nazi concentration camps and is wakened by the hate of a war he survived. She has passed him today, an assemblage of badges he did not understand. But he noticed too clearly the swastika biro-ed on her bag. He takes out the medals and death comes in visions as the missing pieces of his sleep. Bullet holes explode anew and the banter of friends is shot out in last breath epitaphs.

He places them in his pocket, hears collisions chiming, and readies himself in the mirror, straightening his clothes as the young man leaving his hometown for battle. Intellectual reason was always his comfort when he was preparing his arms to kill. He notices the sagging skin, which is a snapshot of an ocean in motion, lolloping down over the tattoo that was a bond to his unit. Wrinkles have the jubilation of survival, yet they map out the lines of lives snuffed out by brutality awarded the nobility of hindsight. He rolls down the shirt, fixes buttons for a uniform and pulls on the heavy jacket not acclimatised to summer.

Outside, the sun bakes mud on a hillside waiting, scratching love messages to those at home with the barrel of his gun. In the air, there are the scattered sounds of operations flickering eyelids behind sunglasses as patients hallucinate in the oblivious ignorance between life and death.

The rhythm of his footsteps makes no dramatic entrance, but instead happens upon a weary beat, waking in apathy for all the characters neglected by society, their lives and tribulations ignored because they don't fit into a marketing strategy. Sometimes, like now, he dares to question what it has all been for: "Life has been unfaithful. And it all promised so so much," becomes an incantation in his head, as regimented as soldiers marching to war, imbued with courage and conviction, convinced by leaders that they are doing good. "I see them still - not only in sleep - all the dead and forgotten, striking matches with their soles, moving in for the kill. And those who survived are now wheeled out once a year to face the hollow applause, cheering the dead and dying, marching feet nailing into a coffin. From a war re-told in glorious fictions, in prosaic history lessons, to emotional exploitation. Cheering relieves guilt and screaming is impotent. No one can see the madness behind the eyes, the pain suffocated by patronising salutes as bestowed and defeated sighs returned.

"I fought in a war when I was not much older than you," he tells the youth for his attention. But the youth, a life under his belt that means nothing but is ambitious for leisure time and leisure time to be filled, cannot connect with him. He's taking in clichés and laughing in the old soldier's face. Bill thinks of a soldier now alone, too old and set in his ways to move out when they started shutting down employment. He lives on postcards, on narratives made up of statements, timing his money to the gas meter to keep warm through the cold.

"You wanna take off that old coat old man, get a bit of the sun. Chill out. Take a holiday. Me and my mates, we're off to Greece on the cheap. Get your pension and come along." The guffawing imbecile invokes no joy from Bill, hissing as the laughing gas evaporates.

Natalie Maines and Jenny Byland are carving history onto a bench. It's their bench, their sanctuary; an inanimate object projecting a presence they strive to fashion as their own.

"Excuse me, can I sit?" he asks, out of breath, taking a position before an answer.

"Hiya, Mr Harris," says Natalie, coolly respectful of the figure she has grown up around.

"Hiya, Mr Harris," repeats Jenny, serving to accentuate some bewilderment too.

"You know, I've know your families for years and years. They are a part of me like I am a part of them." It is arduous for Bill to peel off his jacket, but he needs to lose the discomfort to speak from his heart. "You can't really put your finger on what that bond is, but it's there and it goes back. Y'know, you're granddad went to war, don't you?"

"Yeh," said Natalie, aware that she was the focus of Bill's attention."

Bill inhaled into his pocket, rummaging in asphyxiation, and exhaled out the medals. "See these? They gave me these for the war. They made me feel pretty important when I got them. They had this big ceremony. They were photographs, applause. Face in the papers. It never said anything about killing. We were given them for what they said was 'risking lives so others could be free.' They meant those people around at the time. But they also meant the next generation, and the next, and so on. Do you think that means you?"

Bill took out a handkerchief, uniquely initialled for a vagrant Christmas, *B H* in italic blue, and mopped up beads rolling out years down his forehead. He kept the cloth clenched in his fist, alive to the claustrophobic discomfort suggesting repetition.

"I suppose so," said Natalie. "But we are taking it for granted, is that what you mean?"

"Well, it's just that, when I see your bag, and that swastika there, well, I don't understand it."

"It's just a drawing, it doesn't mean anything. I'm not a Nazi or anything."

"Then, why have it?"

"Haven't I got the freedom to have it?"

"It stands for hate, intolerance. Do you know what the holocaust was?"

"I just like the way it looks, that's all."

"Some people say the holocaust didn't happen, or it was exaggerated," added Jenny, tuned in to conspiracy theories that worked her brain.

"Don't ever doubt it," said Bill emphatically. "When you start doubting it, then you start allowing some types to do it again." He broke off, mopped his brow again and breathed deeply.

"Are you okay, Mr Harris?" asked Jenny, alarmed by the vulnerability gasping through pores.

"It's just a fashion thing, that's all," implored Natalie, feisty with misguided teenage potency.

"I know, I know. You want to rebel, make angry all the adults who run your lives. But," he breathed more calmly. "The swastika represents all those who've been brainwashed to believe in hate and bigotry, those who won't question when someone says why don't we build a gas chamber and kill. It's got nothing to do with individuality, but with accepting what has been told. You need to do some research, get a new fashion symbol. That's all I'm saying."

"What about-" began Natalie, halted by a raised hand.

"It's good that you want to debate and argue, but please, take some time to think, and then come back to me. Now, do me a favour, and just wait a while and help me get on the number twelve bus when it comes."

Natalie and Jenny were enthral to their separateness, stacked up on a house of alternative music and cult literature, which they could quote in a frenzy of righteous affirmation of their outsider credentials. But here, they were silent, awed by death's discernable lurking and the shattering of stereotypes of old age. Bill rested on their bench, took in their adolescent carvings and left them embarrassed by their contribution. They helped him onto the bus with a politeness they could never brag about, and then wandered, accompanied by the symphonic silence of mere oxygen, to a territory on the beach which was also marked as their own: a cave where Stuart Adams was colouring rock with a spray can.

"Hey Stu," shrugged Jenny, "what're you writing on there?"

"Fuck the world my sweet things, with a little Burroughs for desert," he replied nonchalantly, taking approval for granted.

"Let's find our own words Stu," she said, carrying a lost cause to their confines, abstracting philosophies from the waves gentle ushering of contempt.

Bill Harris travelled to town with little to say to the dignitaries who recognised him; pleasantries exchanged allowing him to evaporate into rumination, moulding the sweat from his fingers around the jagged edges of medals. He waited at the bus station, reminded himself of when it was once mere scaffolding and corrugated iron, and when such basic conditions were never complained about. Up on the board, were beaming a collection of numbers for buses, their drivers revving to hit the veins of black and white satellite towns and suburbs. He chose a number that took him into the city, intentions and choices manipulated by resolve and necessity, and perhaps a world-weary despair. Poking into a willing antique shop, he laid his medals on a counter for a magnified eye to ponder:

"Yeh, they're nice. Once you've taken off commission and the like and getting my London guy to find a buyer, there are a few expenses. I can give you about four hundred for the lot. That's a good price, mind. You won't get better."

Bill thought about more graves than his own and took the money in meticulously counted out notes. He had no reason to stay in this foreign and unforgiving land and took the next bus back to where his heart could rest. The bus's motion circulated in rhythmic, automatically repeated beats, time ushered on by electrical impulses to get back to a place to rest. Pauses for thought were coloured by contractions to a past he had released, and as he fumbled the notes in his pocket, regret prompted anxiety, as the knowledge that his world was growing smaller became a tangible reality. He thought of his wife with love, his children with love, his town and his home with a blood beat of necessity. He held his fingers in a lock and thought of the terracing where he belonged, the fibres on interlocking brick by chance bonding homes and lives in experiences, the blood flow of reciprocating experiences sustaining a community not mapped by surveys or statistics or profit and loss. As images of seventy-three years sought prominence in his contemplation, they became too much; each one demanding reason and denouement, feverishly yelping for an encore. Stuck in a blockage, Bill

100

gasped aloud, turned heads with his pain. Most knew him. They knew the name and some scattered history of the man who was having a heart attack and they acted with unified precision to relieve his discomfort and order the bus driver to move hastily to the hospital without any thought for where they might have to be. Attention was drawn to the money listless at his pocket, but the person who took it called immediately on democracy and was voted in with nods, entrusted to pass it onto his wife.

I went with Jayne to visit him whilst his statue slept serenely, tranquillized in thoughts, sustained on a drip, his countenance muscular with the images I knew were sifting inside. I made them audible as I shared with Jayne a scrapbook of experiences. The hour passed swiftly, uncomplicated by selfishness and we were kept distant from grief by hopeful prognosis as we left the ward of wounded preachers.

Sean Patrick was wide-eyed four beds down, glancing at the petitions of pain coagulated on his arm. These abrasions had breathed out and let loose the anguish inside, but some days on from the bleeding death-dare, the relief had a temporality that only served to invigorate feelings regenerating in a corroded womb. He wants to feel a new sensation, wondering about pulling his fingernails out. He'd got too used to the scratches, the scurrying for feeling beneath the skin, the red river of his Art and then looking at roses sent by no one he knew: surplus, someone's job to do it, to cheer up. He doesn't want their fucking love; he wants the pain that means he still exists. He's way passed love, way too far down to throw the sweets and stars of lustful reverie.

"Nothing really makes me happy," is his dead-eyed burden. "What are the flowers for? What do they mean? Someone's killed them for this. You might as well bring me the turf from the local common as bring me these dressed up madams."

He was not the talk on Manic Street, for his achievements were the viscera of fantasies played out in solitary liver spots all around town: in the enclosures of unused bus stops, the too distant benches of beach walks, the skin folds of abandoned buildings. A negligible presence, he was a footnote in gossip, an aside when all other narratives had dried up before the time of departure.

"That lad down the road tried to top himself," fuelled other sympathies searching for reason and led to generalisations that diluted the lad down the road. The courtesy of dismay left them uncomfortable at trying to reach an understanding, then nauseous on the futility, for they did not know him and could not construct meaning from the fragments of sightings and hearsay.

Natalie Maines, Jenny Byland and Stuart Adams sought to give Sean more purpose, their talk curiously fascinated and excited by the iconic perfection of suicide:

"Like a rock star, I suppose," offered Stu, spraying *R.I.P.* for symmetry on the cave wall. "Like all these rock stars of nature, stuck in the gloom."

"I spoke to him a few times, but he didn't say much. He didn't seem to have any friends," said Natalie. "Maybe he didn't mean to go all the way."

"We should get him to join our gang when he's better," said Jenny. "Make a space for him on the wall to write his thoughts."

"Yeh," added Stu. "Maybe Bill Harris can have a space too?"

"Don't joke about it," said Natalie, agitated by conscience. "He's alright, he is." She looked down at her bag, at the spot where a swastika was now encircled and divided by an uncompromising slash. "He's more a revolutionary than Sean Patrick will ever be; more than all the phoney rock stars we think are our heroes. Rock's conscience is more like convenience, more like self-promotion. I'd swap all my shitty albums for Plath and Pinter any day."

"Every time you see these bands and singers and celebrities getting together for charity, you always think, well, why don't you give the poor some of *your* money?" said Jenny.

"Right," added Stu. "Conscience is good marketing tool isn't it? Quick, stop fucking your groupies, taking your drugs and counting your cash, you're on stage and the world is looking. It must be time to down instruments and push a wheelchair into a camera, spill some crumbs for Africa."

"It's in the news, so it's got to be cool. This week, for charity, we're spreading AIDS. No time for cancer, it's been around too long. It's old news. You'll have to wait until it becomes a retro fashion thing," spat out Jenny.

The fluidity of words, torn from incipient experience and cultural wreckage, splattered on cave walls in garish colours and stuttering handwriting. As they ran dry of ideas, the intellectual recycling disintegrated to a symphony of tourettes; anger throwing out the flotsam and jetsam of half-formed theories. They stretched a path along Manic Street towards the library for a fix, passing the preachers sunning themselves on foreign lands pock-marked by explosions. Tonsil clouds drift ethereally in a mumble, murmuring machine-gun fire setting neighbour against neighbour, and the seeds of life once haphazardly scattered across divides turn into poisonous gasses to terminate races. Through the capillaries of Manic Street, ethnic cleansing makes all such good Europeans as blind eyes shut out the blaze of the sun.

Here in town, there is the nucleus of a wider canvas, sliding into disrepair through ignorance and grief. Lisa Burnham wanders with the weight of a new life tormenting her glands. She pushes about Anthony, to seek the relief of sleep, for a moment when she can add up an excess of "love you" to mean something significant, not just repeated in imitations she seeks to resist. Now she is mother, she is closer than ever to the figure that bore her, wrapped up in innocent thrills she tries hard to retrieve. And yet, she will always return to the etiolating of her social security room, squashed into Manic Street's terrace with memories of her elapsed experience. She lives in the home where she was neglected with ease and runs through the mistakes she feels destined to make. She is mummified in snapshots, theoretically aroused in poses, saving the cash in hand-jobs and blowjobs to escape her tomb.

She is sustained by the drip-feed of concern, the approximated helpfulness of neighbours who say, "Leave him with me and have a break."

"So I walk to all the nowhere places I have grown to loathe, all the rumps around town where thoughts shit on me. The break is so lonely. I miss Anthony too much. He is all I feel close to and the only thing with an unconditional response. So I walk to pass time, like I've got a life to go to, mark clock-hands with a fantasy of existence before returning to his comfort. I feel a landslide of debris from a past rising up, chasing me towards the fissures of circumstances where life support is pert tits and didactic overtime. Only when I am done, cleaned up, returned to my baby, do I dare to take a glimpse into another future. He holds my finger in the palm of his hand, gargles non-commercial monosyllables that concentrate the moment and shut off the sounds wearily swelling on the street below."

"She does porn up there, gets them out on the cheap. I've seen her in magazines spread out for juices," comes from a male who works for a man. "She's not bad. I'm thinking of offering her a tenner for a shag." His gloating glotals grate on phlegm, spit out the superiority of a man with money in his pocket, which he pisses away on weekends and on cheap flights to cheap sunshine venues where he drinks the same beer and gets browned under the same sun. He's superior when his faculty with spastic words attracts women for fractions of pleasure and ultimately the boredom that loses him a mate. He laughs it off with clichés of "plenty more fish in the sea," and such like and fills in his own time with porno mags. He is superior again, over the static women he controls with one hand and obliterates with the other. His name is Jimmy Best. It's one of his lines: "Jimmy Best, darling, and you can bet I am the best." He wouldn't know irony if it was licking its lips and beckoning him towards an open crotch. He's lived in town all his life and has developed immunity to the lives of others.

"Shut up," says Gary Orton, diseased by a friendship from youth and the need of a drinking gang to raise its collective I.Q. "Why don't you leave it out? She's all right. I bet she's only doing it for her kid."

"Whoa! Gaz fancies her then. Well, buddy; you might get a reduced rate if that's the case."

"Y'know Jimmy, I wonder why you don't hang on to your girlfriends. I mean, with such charm."

"Hey, don't be so touchy! When was your last shag?"

"About the same time as your last wank, no doubt."

"Hey, why don't you marry her, you touchy bastard? God, you do need a shag off her."

"Grow up, Jimmy. Just have a *little bit* of sensitivity when it comes to women. You know, we left the cave millions of years ago, you can stop acting like a bloody ape."

Stranded by imbecility, Jimmy put a fist out in retort, took the wind in a swing and sent Gary crashing to the ground. They tumbled like the condemned buildings bellowing dust under the wrecking balls around town.

Mikey and Danny Madison intervened to separate the jutting chests frantic to regain pride. A commotion of words inflicted further pathetic pains, but eventually both Gary and Jimmy turned away from each other and from lifetimes wed by chance. Closing statements offered nothing new, merely throwaway curses from a predictable archive of priapic antagonism.

Danny was back in town to see Bill Harris, Mikey briefly returning for a family visit.

"Another little battle neither won nor lost. You see it all the time in town centres at weekends up and down the country," said Danny. "It doesn't add up to much when you compare it to Bosnia and Croatia."

"You haven't given up on politics then, Danny?"

"It seems a bit late to become apathetic. Anyway, the tide is turning. The country's sick of the Tories now, ready for a change. I've travelled a lot over the last few years, like I was trying to rid myself of the endemic self-interest of this society. Jesus, I've seen some poverty and exploitation you would not believe. People are being persecuted, tortured and murdered in foreign lands and western governments are turning a blind eye. Now that I'm back, I'm ready to pick up the fight again. You can feel something in the air that suggests this country's ready for change."

"It seems I've heard that before somewhere."

"I suppose you've switched to the Tories now you've got your own business?" Danny joked.

"I don't think so. But, anyway, nowadays the Labour Party means little to people like me. Look at my Dad. He's voted Labour all his life, and they haven't done anything to help him."

"I wouldn't argue with that. They don't care about places like here. We have always elected Labour, so their attitude is, why bother? I've seen it from the inside. All their campaigns now are about winning Middle England marginals. They'll tell them whatever is needed to get their vote. So you can forget about taxes to help public services, about returning national industries to the country, about unions having any power to help the working people. But, I guess, anything gives more hope than the same lot of sleazy thieves getting in again. You think about people like Bill Harris with a lifetime of service to the country and to community, and what is he doing in his retirement? Selling war medals, making do with a pitiful pension, watching an ugly world replace the one he knew. What's his legacy? Idiots on catwalks in London and Milan, wearing war medals as accessories to some freak show costume."

"How's Bill doing?" asked Mikey.

"He's talking. He says he's going to be my campaign manager for the next election. He's a battler, that's for sure. Y'know what he's like. He's asking about Ray Young, talking about how lucky he's been compared to people like Ray. His outlook, as always, is about wanting to help others. You just don't see the like of him much anymore. He asked about Eddie too. He's heard he's been unwell."

"News gets around here doesn't it? Dad's getting old too. You never really realise it until you go months without seeing the face you've grow up with. You get accustomed to not noticing the invisible changes. A life down the pit is catching up with him. Thank god our Pete's around. I feel pretty guilty at times."

"Come on, Mike, he's proud you've made something of yourself, and Pete too. He's got plenty for good company around here." Danny looked down Manic Street. "It seemed so big once. Never thought I'd be standing here imbibing cloth-cap nostalgia, but you know, we're as delicate as any generation whose youth had a place to flourish. The memories have a potency you feel protective of, so you become someone who laments change, well, just because it is change."

"Too may empty houses now, Danny. I've heard they're planning to knock the whole block down for regeneration. I see they're building something on the old mine now."

"A store of some sort, but I've asked many times and nobody's giving anything away. They know it'll just be another kick in the eye to all those people whose lives revolved around the pit."

The bruised tired lips of the preachers are still receptive, still sending out ripples of dialogue to unify the world, clanking skeletal meanings from who said what to whom and how it threaded a tissue of details to flesh out the whole. From the superficial and temporal, the cavities of chatter are filled and new dawns spark arteries kept alive through night-before tales. For all those accessories still preaching there is the skin-shedding certainty that neighbours will throb with second-hand descriptions like the enema of Art, throwing out veins to cells of relatives pocketed around town. This battered town, weighed with blame and the finely tuned jealousies running sore from capitalism's catch-all grasp, still thrives on inherent connections maintained by elders and the families of former workers, and those who know others who once made a claim to community. The town's infrastructure was not yet eaten by commerce, instead still breathing on the lives of people like Bill Harris.

"Knuckle down," was preached with venom from both left and right. One rapped the fingers stretching out for measly much, the other formed a fist and a finger and a fuck you to the world.

"Anger is an energy. Anger is an energy!" Danny Madison beat the drum into the guts of places of despair, into longitudinal, circular and oblique layers of lives where the cigar-chompers of government never did venture. Only in Danny, possessing an idealism bruised yet elastic in its healing capability, could there still be the brittle innocence of misunderstanding the forces at work in this perverted new evolution of the species. When he felt the reciprocation of the people who gave time and made space in their antiquated larder cupboards, he sensed change as fluid as embryos chartering the progress of typical time. He read the press for contractions, saw the softening of those around the country whose dreams had grown hardened in negative equity, and watched opinion polls dilating as they swung away from the right. On the surface the Labour Party was the only party that could change the government and it now seemed to be engaging those who'd once bought into the Tory ideal. "A change is gonna come," popped hopeful and fizzy and made those cynical doubters dizzy.

But, at bus stops, there were full stops where the bandwagon was without wheels, having to put up and shut up and fix on a spot for defence. This was a party that the working class were not invited, instead they were just hastily tossed placebo-promises to take the spots of discolouring questions, leaving necks on the breadline to wilt on crucifix crosses. The push for delivery makes us shit ourselves, and the walking abortions are too busy breathing for life to sit up and smell. Manic Street has fight, its people have passion, but for the moment they keep it quiet, or else sell it to the unwashed who might just scrub their hands to vote in marginal-pelvis.

6
HOLLOW

The infested summer of 1993 was fired with catalysts sparked by love running through streets, dropping excess oil on canvasses, discolouring palates so that sweet-tasting emotions camouflaged uncertainty and a prosaic procession of corrosion. The primacy of lust and limitless energy of reciprocated feelings transported perspectives to a more beautiful place where Romanticism could flourish, and indeed be accentuated by the tangled debris of physical and emotional disintegration.

With Jayne Atkinson, there was a love to neglect time, marked only by adventurous explosions, which shook our frames under lamp-lit security and chased devils into shadows for ephemeral thrills. We were irresistible in arteries, bleeding passion to shake and wake streets grown old and weary. We were of the purist innocence in our exploration of the present, standing on hairs, chilled only by awe.

This was a destructive love, arms wrapped in stranglehold. She has a beauty that crushes me, makes me want to open my skin as an act of expression that my inarticulate thoughts cannot convey. She is beautiful like an obsession, so that when I bleed she infects me more, makes me child in my devotion and all that that state of mind cannot take. I am in the shadow of her love so that I no longer see clearly, nor am I able to think with reason. Each time she sucks me in I imagine her absence one day, and when I confront her with my jealousies it only makes us more brittle, makes my flesh rip, makes the day drip, makes us distant at dawn.

I walk around the deserted streets of this town, suffering in love, but I have no awareness of how she suffers too. I will only see when hindsight fills an impenetrable distance between us. Within the currents of absence, I will keep making her fragile and be blind to her suffering.

It burned out before we could even see those last magnificent sunsets of the season. Not for us the satisfaction of uncoiling breathlessly at the distant pains of our labour. For us, there surfaced the infantile erosion of insults and accusations as we separated back to our unhinged orbits. We were amputated in an instant, scratching out the skin of images processed by senses raw for reasons that were never going to be apparent.

I was still watching a firework's last glow, whilst out of my vision the ground soothed in lessening heat to wear its new scar.

You could ask then why they closed the pit when the ground was still pregnant with resources and the country still needed the fuel and the labour, but cerebral impulses were already way ahead of the moment of realisation, impulsively punching out commands mocking voluntary movements. Why I grazed my knuckles, I do not know, but I shattered glass and splintered wood for the fun of still knowing I existed, and somehow it gave me control.

I existed in stasis, weighted time by my conscious noting of its passage, to twilight evenings when shadows joined me for company. These fiends of contemplation chatted inconsequential anecdotes about the new lover who'd taken Jayne from this town for a life with stick-figure scrawls and shopping list itineraries. Last I heard – from Paul, a friendship renewed – she was engaged to a denouement I could only sketch in fat, loathsome caricatures.

Through autumn and winter she would not disappear as I let experiences bleed into my arms with my pathetic beer can slashes. During this time, Dad had a tumour removed, drawing love to his convalescence as some obscene escape. I hugged him like childhood, spilled salty tears between the cracks of bonds I had neglected or took for granted.

Ray Young dedicated a song to him as he returned to the stage: "This is for Eddie, who's been a part of me since we all were born here. And to my son, Johnny, whose life was not a waste, this is for him too, and the people who've helped me fill the space. Thanks to Pete Thornby, the man on the drums; the backbone of our ageing and ramshackle band. Thanks to Dickie Chadwick, whose bass is this band's heartbeat, and to George Lewis on the keyboard; our bones and our body. A Merry Christmas to you all. Here's an oldie..."

The cheering crowd were not there to notice the hesitancy in the band's rusty beginning, but were more keen instead to re-live glory days and re-new alliances, singing along with each chorus and chiming drinks in between banter. Each band member went through emotions, slowly stitching together the body of sounds to find the grooves of fingerprints plucking and pummelling and holding onto notes for impressions of experiences. This pocket of restricted activity unified the stale resistance to mockery in irony and made no apologies for re-living obsolete history. The world outside the social club froze out the sterile progression of retro fashion, offering no profit for image-makers in fashionable places working out how to re-package the innocence of those with disposable stigmatas.

A seasonal encore sent them all outside happy, winding their ways and wares homewards through the sobriety of the season's climate; the club's little republic merely transplanted to Manic Street for lamp-lit theatre.

Honour flourished in hands held across icy concrete, stopping off for chattering accelerated by nature. Gary Orton's at Lisa Burnham's door, clinching nervously as he resuscitates her faith in men. They have stood here several times, unsure, like fingers-crossed, hands-locked teens at the threshold of desire. She hasn't been unclothed for profit for some months now and has grown accustomed to modesty and how it has allowed her to grow.

"That was good night Gary, thanks."

"You don't need to thank me, Lisa, I love being with you."

"You've been so understanding and patient. Last time Anthony was sleeping away, and I went in alone, I spent most of the night awake, just thinking about mistakes and doubts, letting them spin around. I felt lonely, but each time I imagined you with me, some old memories came back and kept telling my heart to back off. But at the same time, I've never been so happy."

"You don't have to explain Lisa. I know how men can hurt. My Dad fucked off when I was fourteen, for a woman half his age, and then drank a way back into our lives when she left him. We watched him try to drag us all down, until he fucked off again for good, giving mum a few bruises and me a crack on the skull. She was getting drunk enough not to feel it. After that, I didn't want anyone to be with her again. Most people don't know the hate in love."

"Come in," Lisa said, a smile shivering parts of her face, elevating and levitating across contours so long unmoved.

Their fumbling emanations, transient puffs of naturally cooled ardour, dispersed before the doorway's light fused. Several bolts choked out troubles and drew attention from other preachers on Manic Street.

"I'd like to think it was the music that brought them together," said George Lewis.

"Ah, he's a good lad," said Ray Young, collared by a poignant image of his son, and rubbing his chin aggressively to push back its quiver. "Let's say it was the music and sleep on that."

"It all felt really good tonight, Ray. You never lose it do you?"

"It's in our souls George. Good night."

In thrown-away chip wrappings, souls were departing, blurred between lines greased with that week's sleaze. Obituaries were chosen to fit the word count in columns near the section on births. Each one, a good soul, now effortlessly with the angels and undiscerning gods, and ridden with the narrow vocabulary of sentimental indulgence. Their lives outlasted the cremations that were cheaper and more manageable, sitting in yearning urns in dusty rooms so some part of their souls could remain, by turns trapped and resuscitated.

Natalie, Jenny and Stu were analysing Kurt Cobain, playing out songs in the cave as they held a vigil for meaning. Initially excited by the drama of suicide, they flicked admiration on walls, tearing apart the corpse of a pop album for vicarious suffering. Eventually, through systematic evaluation, they would step out to the waves, repulsed by such affectation.

"Daniel Webster said 'Suicide is confession'," stated Stu. "Kurt must be telling us he had nothing left and so he just gave up."

"Another rock cliché, then?" pondered Natalie as all three faced out to tease the waves. "I hate all the exploitation that goes with celebrity death."

"We are as guilty as anyone, dwelling on its magnificence," interrupted Jenny. "Fuck all that shit. Kurt had a beautiful, fragile soul. I'm going to pretend that *Bleach* and *Nevermind* and *In Utero* never reached out to millions, that they were only heard by a small cult, and heard by them with intensity."

The other two concurred.

"What would it be like if we all just walked in now and drowned ourselves?" asked Stu. "You think we'd make any front pages?"

"Yeh," replied Natalie. "We'd make the local paper and some of the nationals. We'd get on the television news too, probably more time on satellite and cable channels. They'll be wringing their hands and pointing fingers at rock music and immoral cultural influences. And just when most have forgotten us, they knock out a documentary on Channel Four, finding some angle that fits in with the footage they have already shot. Then we'd be forgotten again, except by the few anaemic teenage Goths who'd come to this spot with their cheap liquor and fags and salute our deaths."

"Just like us then," added Stu.

They all laughed, attracting the attention of a figure walking along the beach. Sean Patrick changed direction and went another way, fearful of the crowd who'd spoken to him as like minds but were too alive in self-confidence to connect with.

"Hey, there's Sean," said Jenny, waving through the suffocation of distance. "Sean!" dissipated upon rolling waves. "Guess he doesn't want to see us."

"He was into Nirvana," said Stu. "I shudder to think what he makes of Cobain's suicide."

"Perhaps they are kindred spirits, only separated by exposure and indulgence."

"When you talk to Sean Patrick, you realise we are just acting out this disaffection and alienation. We've got each other, but he's got nothing."

The conversation returned to death and found epithets for the famous and worthless, homeless and hungry. Talk on Manic Street or any street is animated by mortality; feverish with assimilations that will add up to an eloquent evocation of a life well spent. Will stocks have risen sufficiently to throw up a chiselled summary that will be blasted by ages but still cause pause for thought in future wanderers?

Nothing becomes populations like death; levelling emotion to a cloying paralysis, a homogenous grief discharged with the desperation that it will equate to our own. Media belly-scratchers sink nails into guts and pull out bygone eras where celebrity death is revived and coated with the edits of images timed to mellow music. Each time, we seem to feel it more, as if we were there when John Lennon was shot. The message is that we *must* have felt something, just *must* have shed a tear. If we don't have an anecdote then we haven't even lived.

Labour leader John Smith died of heart attack on 12th May. Even those on Manic Street who'd grown tired of the Labour Party congregated at a special church service to pay their respects, before moving to the social club.

Bill Harris, receiving the love of those who hadn't seen him out for nearly a year, paid tribute to a silent room:

"Comrades, first of all I'd like to make a personal thank you to all those people who have given me their time, help and kind words as I recovered over the past year. There have been many and it has been a powerful testament to the sense of community that still exists in this town. I have been humbled by the selflessness of others. It's true to say that we take it for granted these days because we've always had it, but we seem to live in an age where the individual has become more important and social cohesion has become a phrase more likely to be cast in political mudslinging as an aspersion."

Bill paused, allowed "Here, here," to circulate without the usual House of Commons vacuity.

"John Smith always seemed a man above such ya-boo politics. At a time when working people feel they have no voice, he was a man still speaking for us. He probably seemed a little out of place, believing in social justice and wealth redistribution at a time when those in government are more concerned with keeping the rich wealthy and scoff at caricatures of working class life. He gave many people hope that the next government will be Labour and end the shame of fifteen years of selfish misrule. His legacy is that we can still have that hope. He was a solid man in whom we could place our trust. It'll take someone special – someone I can't yet identify – to cement that sense of belief and hope. I speak for all in this club when I say that we feel an enormous sense of tragedy that the work he began cannot be completed without his vision. Let us spend a moment to remember John Smith and give thanks for his compassion."

Bill led the unplanned contemplation as figures watched the spaces where no eyes could distract.

"God bless him," from Bill, prompted a cheer from the gathering, not just for John Smith, but for Bill Harris too.

Many people hugged Bill, including Danny Madison, who had rejoined the Labour Party during John Smith's leadership and been selected as the next candidate for the constituency.

"Good to see you out and about Bill," he said, tearful in his embrace. "I think you're right about the legacy. We still have hope."

Naturally, the positives would snap into symmetry of rage, not quelled by the decorum of the occasion, Danny Madison fuelled by the impatience of seeing out John Major's second term:

"The Tories have a good line in fake sympathy, but it's pretty nice for them that the papers aren't filled with stories about Nicholas Scott anymore. This vile MP admits misleading Parliament when he's trying to block a bill to outlaw discrimination against the disabled, and he's on the verge of being forced out, and then he's off the hook, gleefully unpopular on presses and keeping his seat. He's a worthless shit, and he's one of many in the Tory party. He'll get his next election, media interest or no media interest."

The zeitgeist is a blitzkrieg of fashions and interests, and flavours on the palate are matter-of-fact, prosaic with a dead-eyed conviction; hating purity, wanting everything corrupt. On Manic Street the air is always salty, seasoning emotions with bitterness at some clearly defined 'other' existence, partying as "lads" purely Thatcherite in perspective. For this is the endgame. Images of happiness don't transmit to Manic Street. On the television they may be winning their millions and eating their celebrity, but on Manic Street there's a reality far more challenging – staying alive.

Sean Patrick wrestles with his thoughts, his depression muscular and in control from years of engagement. He has not let himself be corrupted by happiness, but now, long after the thrill has gone, now he misses the things he took for granted. He delivers an archaic cool in his addressing of "baby" and "honey," loaded up on irony as this summer's fashion accessory, but it barely masks the insecurity beneath. This is his self-disgust, splattered across walls, dripping from the books, from Miller to Mailer, Plath to Pinter. He's tied up in knots of contradictions, wanting not to be what was expected, then too distant from the purity of innocence, from a time when he seemed to know what he wanted, what he felt, how to express it. Now he can only cling to the emptiness of believing in nothing:

"But it is my nothing," he yells. "I am the generation that has become obliterated with sensations. We could deal with things but we prefer to blank them out so that virtually every atrocity doesn't have that much impact any more. I hear 'fuck you, weirdo' or am mocked from open spaces. I am all of an ideology that is all about 'don't say nigger and we'll forget all about British slavery'. My sensitivity is politically correct, worn as a gag on my mouth, ripping my flesh with a forced smile of acceptance. I am the creep, the minority, the untouchable outsider, the bitch, the whore, the malevolent loner."

Walking home from the hospital, again, he has taken the roses as a kind of joke, to himself. It's always to an audience of one: the most appreciative and critical. And his laughter is bitter, self-conscious, forced; just like his sleep is endurance where thoughts crowd into, a procession of butchers splitting his reason.

Once more staring at the ceiling, once more the dirty splatters of his insides mark time on the walls.

"I've been too honest with myself, I should have lied like everybody else." He felt a dichotomised snap. He has nobody to lie to. He feels like the Devil, like the son and heir, like all the regrets and possibilities and abortions that rattle around infinity searching for completion, or mirrors for self-deception.

So damn easy to cave in that he hates himself for even contemplating it, for even being so vulgarly weak and obvious.

This is his yesterday and his tomorrow. He determines never to have convalescing roses again.

"I hate purity, hate sanctimonious rhetoric; hate all the emptiness that comes with rumination. I sit in a room and gut my emotions for feeling, reach inside with feisty fingers and find only timid, unpluckable bone. In the mirror, my true self protruding through my sunken coating, boring the replica with self-esteem sucking in."

The rag and bone man still hollers his trade around these undernourished streets, chiming out in lilting, submissive repetitions the definition of his employment like a death-rattle confession announcing a plague on all these anorexic edifices.

"Society needs to condemn a little more and understand a little less," said John Major.

Through the veneer of redemption, Marcus Bowles is a hangman writing off lives and experiences in sums to make a profit: "The investment is so low and the risk practically non-existent. The land is cheap and, with the government grants, it'll cost very little to build new houses and turn a profit. It's a sea-front location for God's sake! The people who live around would be more than happy to take the money and run away from these disastrous places."

"Rag-bone! Rag-bone!" coughs over creaking wheels, punctuated by pauses when a door opens, chucking out the much-chewed and sucked-dry clutter of the gristle of annual ceremonies.

They've skinned parts of town and left souvenir pamphlets, printed on local presses for circulation amongst the ageing, glossy with sepia and black and white images of how we used to like to live. In paradox it feeds a sense of stability, resurrecting labour pains and idylls from seasons when the senses urgently functioned.

Captioned climaxes caught in a snapshot suggest places where families found a moment. On these streets, at the foreground of these buildings, consciousness dented a presence, spoke and tasted, inhaled and sent glory through veins and cells, fed possibilities through the grey matter of concrete and steel. Interconnections were formed, pulsing for milliseconds, consolidating awareness and storing it for breathless reawakening slumped out on couches at Christmas.

Sean Patrick touches such moments, feels their rawness through distance, and regurgitates the happiness of innocence to wash away through systems. He is rags and bone, riddled with literary literals, fattened by the mask of abstruse metaphors, readying his carcass for some impending day's ink.

None of the thoughts emanating through gestures and expressions on Manic Street offered a hint or a wink or a half-hearted sigh for what was to come. The characters circulating paving and tarmac and condemnation of plywood were too busy threading together the nerve fibres of the present to even know Sean Patrick for more than a passing aside.

Lisa Burnham was busy practising love, finding the unity of a complicated family structure thoughtlessly denounced by the Tory cocksuckers running the country. George Lewis played the Bossa Nova on his organ, shuffling optimism from side to side, calling on Ray Young for a jam between houses being written up in profitable slices. There am I too, counting the costs of self-publication for a book of images concerned with lives diseased by neglect. My thoughts are with Bill Harris and a dedication in preface, and I am drunkenly invigorated by the changes they might ring.

Dad's downstairs, coughing convalescence, flicking through amateur archetypes stitched into time. Sean Patrick is a fleeting presence in the bedroom agitation of Natalie Maines' scrawls, but she, like Jenny Byland and Stu Adams, is too involved in the fire of her own soul to resist the phantasmagoria possibilities of an infinite canvass of possibilities.

Sean bled himself in a present delayed, growing pale through hours when plans were being made and the summer sun was cheering for the people.

"All virgins are liars, honey," says Marcus Bowles with an arrogance patronising the lives he was strangulating. "In these plagued streets of pity you can buy anything." He celebrates being despised when pissing in continental streets, ravaging innocence by signatures on documents. "I've made more money in a week than most make in a year. If you want to succeed you'd better fill your guts with this passion." So much masturbation, he slices the flesh off real emotion. He's got a job to do, but there's a glee in the numbers he crunches when adding up the profits involved in buying up properties on Manic Street. But deep within, the duality tears him apart, and he still fears sleep; an imagined whack from his dad feels real in dreams. He can't shout, can't scream, and is knotted with anguish in trying but not daring to express pain.

He can't tell his colleagues (he has no friends – "Everyone I've loved or hated always seems to leave") so he counts the numbers, thinks of it as some kind of Blue Peter appeal where the target is enough money to get his cock cut off, to be virgin again.

"Yeh, I can get you whatever you want. Everything has a price," tunes from him as it has done for nearly a decade. But it's an old philosophy, one that now rings ever more hollow, one that is now little more than a mask, like the plywood being hammered into the former homes of former families. He sees the connection, feels some regret even though his pre-occupation is the self: self-hate, self-pity, and the past that made him a mess, so that the ghosts of broken families work mostly as reminders.

Sean Patrick passed on and passed through in swiftness unbecoming on any life. By morning, there was the business of grief and the totalitarianism of obituaries, nauseous with the certainty that a choice had been fulfilled.

They mulled over his ghost and blind articulations flapping at all the imagined light from a life working through double entry inside a coffin, consoling themselves with best-fitting eulogies. Lodged into moments *The Holy Bible* is arbitrary yet eloquent. Here are cries for a childhood too far gone. Here is an album septic with sepia-tinged memories and a conviction that beyond childhood innocence there is only turmoil and ultimately death. There is no chance of reconciliation because all dreams are counterfeit. A cracked syntax is freezing by the clock's unanimous authority. We are here to mourn through perfunctory ceremony with emotions emptied by agony.

The iniquitous sun reminds mourners of innocence; of places where throwing sticks in streams protected the players from doubt, lusty on recreation without boundaries. The subdued talk snatches moments from the finiteness of reality, barely sustained on morsels of memories. Each anecdote wheezes on the pollen-heavy breeze, blasted through breathless to make a name for the dead boy. For those outside the darkened essence, there is no fascination with Sean Patrick, no need to analyse the chronology of where a life went under. He hasn't touched lives like a history of killers. Rather than floating on shoulders to anonymity's hollow, he should have been splattered on papers with notoriety as his eternal bedfellow. Sutcliffe and Dahmer, Bundy and Milosevic; all have their purposes printed on the bruised prose of news. They've got their respect and wait in time for irony to elevate their murder to cultish glamour. Not Sean Patrick, sensitive in shadows, peeling his flesh in rag and bone beckoning.

"Why did he have to die so young?"

"It's such a waste."

"Why doesn't someone put a hole in Thatcher's arteries?"

Even in death, his presence fades to the peripherals, animated only as a prompt for more pressing concerns.

"Genocide is alive and well all around this brutal planet. Lives are extinguished for being born on the wrong side of organised lines, or for challenging governments who quell questions through the barrel of a gun. I see media finger-fuckers sucking the bones of the carnage of serial killers, dwelling on psychosis like it's *the* end of the millennium drug to fix on to. American society, gratified by cathode ray fame, feeds on the achievements of murderers, because celebrity is the narcotic of the age. In it there is the pride of belonging, of slaughtering numbness for some grotesque sense of being; of existing, of leaving a mark on histories flipping through channels." Danny Madison was rampant with words to rage against fashions. "Kill for glory, kill for peace, join the holocaust and wait for sound bite bait. Might as well preach extinction and have the flies for an audience. Governments wring hands and ponder on plans to end the genocide being beamed around the world, but it's all of front, these washing palms of guilt, for these are the same claws that once pressed flesh with dictators, selling them weapons and turning a blind eye to carnage. You know who the real mass murderers are? Try Ronald Reagan, Margaret Thatcher, George Bush, John Major, Bill Clinton. Be shocked by the chaos in the former Yugoslavia, but then take a close look at the unmarked graves festering reminders in Central America. In Grenada, Haiti, El Salvador and Nicaragua, you'll find the poisonous effects of Western intervention. American-backed murder squads have spread democratic-death in an unstylish and media-unfriendly manner. I don't see it on front pages, or under the urgent bombast of television news headlines. Where aren't the talking heads dissecting this history?"

I listened and concurred with, "Our culture is being poisoned by Americanisation. As we run through the decades as apathetic as the wilting of flowers, we are only alive to our own mortality, stabbing about in blindness to hook in and drain the carcass of popular culture. The futility of our lives, not tempered by Belsen or Auschwitz, is instead diluted – even goddam saved – by the business of show business and the calling of gravestones. I think people have been left so light-headed by the rampages of capitalism and consumerism that they are now waking to the fact that they have nothing of substance to show. So all that remains is a vicarious re-enactment of what was trendy at some vague point in their lives. If you couldn't be there, you must at least have stuffed your face with crisps when the event was being broadcast. That's enough for an epitaph."

"I look down Manic Street and see a rich tapestry of experiences, able to renew and flow in transfusions through generations. I don't take it for granted that I was born here, that my grandparents were born here and that during our time on the street stories were exchanged that kept yesteryears alive. I know the lives of others by chance, but it is not something ephemeral. It stays with me and I want to pass it on to."

"I think it'll get knocked down now. The wheels are in motion. Some of our neighbours are tempted by the prices being offered, and you can't blame them. Opportunities are at a dead end on streets like this, destined to only exist in tongues."

"So, we fight it, we frustrate the likes of Marcus Bowles and pressure him into giving up, going somewhere else for his profits. Believe me Pete, I know the process, and it can take years for permissions, and there are plenty of appeals to clog up the arteries. Whatever happens, we won't go without a fight."

I paused to cut off the vitriol, uneasy in the moment I was turning up to present: "Have you looked through the book, then?"

"Yes. It's fantastic Pete. It's powerful, touching, persuasive. The pictures could speak for themselves, but what you have written gives them soul. Don't be embarrassed; I know what you are leading up to. I'd be glad to give you some money to get it published. Is it looking likely?"

"I think it is. Mum left me a bit, which I haven't touched, and Mikey is going to give me some money too. Bill Harris is going to be a sponsor, and Ray Young and the band."

"Well good luck. It's important, and I'm sure it'll make a difference. Count me in."

Lent such trust, I was shaking for clarity through weeks of preparation, determined to perspire for sobriety and dignity. Turning new leaves was a past time of my class:

self-destructiveness tormented by the need for escape. Out of our heads weekends stumbled towards the finality of passive Sundays, ashamed of excess, purging the system for routines ingrained. Only the cruelty of unemployed Mondays could drag the self back to a fractious intolerance of existing in the margins. New leaves atrophied and were crushed upon the cruelty of seasons, reaching the end game of resurrection in festive last chances.

Too often there is a reason to celebrate or commiserate, stuttering for a conclusiveness that is fat with optimism in epilogue, bleary-eyed and bored in prologue before sneaking into the appendix of miscellaneous addictions for the acceptance of fatalism (albeit predicated on some barely defined date when the process will start again).

Manic Street and the lives therein offer a bypass in the process, the crumbling homes frosted with the pathetic natural processes that erode and shuffle onwards. So, wandering limbs of families alight from their comfort to hand deliver approximations of glad tidings, ticked off on notepads eliminating the names of those still abiding; by a code and rhetoric still visceral with communality.

In boxes of forty cards, eight differentiated clones, cheapened in a supermarket, which is the butt of shameful jokes. But those who give and those who receive barely notice the appearance, sticking with spittle for connection in the hasty greetings and indomitable names that will spark some dried out old tale.

Some of these cards fell through the letterbox where my childhood friend Andy had grown. But they would never be opened, and they were not cashed in on the monarch's authority to garner the effort of sending on. Andy was long gone, and since November he had little cause to visit Manic Street as his parents had sold up and moved away.

Such departures grow more poignant through their silent inevitability. Preceded without a celebratory send off, they leave with weighty sacks of sorrow, brief handshakes and hugs and decadent shrugs, emotions all priced-out.

Tatty decorations flinch on shop fronts, teething on the wind, chortling jovially to dim bulbs strapped around the town centre's tottering Christmas tree. The annual ritual remains imbued with an effort and a spirit where the inhabitants can loosen language and shake out ideas of forgiveness and conscience and provincial goodwill to all humanity. Dispelled on the high street are skeletal stalls chiming out tinny tunes from the trinkets and toys animated by air, where opportunists shout out prices irresistibly frugal. All items are immediate, imperative; gasping through the count down of shopping days, offering savings on items whose durability is ephemeral.

"These sell for thirty quid in most shops, but I'm not asking that. I'm not asking twenty quid or ten quid. I'm giving it away for a fiver."

"The last of the stock, there's no more after this."

"It's two for the price of one."

"Buy one, get one free."

Echoing in parody of a preening capitalist ethos, these individuals drift from ceremonies searching for the angles in fashions, for room at the inn of Immaculate Conception, where loose change buys in bulk the counterfeit materials selling in frenzies at places in Middle England's belly. Deception is not their intention, as the buyers know too well what is being offered. These gifts are merely stocking fillers easing the burden of expectation, wrapped up in thin seasonal paper, birthed as gifts to make able participation in the ritual.

Dickie Chadwick has a stall creaking with coin, supplementing an income drained of redundancy, where playing in a band now draws from not only passion but also necessity. He got his stock from a man who travels the region in an uninsured white van, who got it from a man who owns a warehouse and drives a Jaguar and takes stock from Asian enigmas. Somewhere in the chain, the arteries run to a factory where cheap labour bloodies its fingers for a pittance over more hours than sleep.

"I don't know what it is," he tells dallying clients huddling for a display, "but it's what all the kids want. I've tried them out and they work okay. They're just as good as the ones in the shops, but you won't get ripped off with the price."

He freezes through unspecified hours and collects his pension in a sack, counting it out at home to warm his fingers before practice, then taking out his bass guitar and strumming satisfaction and other covers for the night, enveloping his wife with those still-skilled hands.

In the idiom of our history, hand shakes bid "all the best," for Christmas and beyond, to neighbours and former colleagues, to the man who delivers the milk and the shopkeeper whose continued survival marks a stand against the times.

"All the best, Tommy," is not isolated, nor empty, nor exclusive to the season. It is said to reinforce bonds that stay urgent through daily interaction. This goodness is not forced, nor the last cries of a dangling man, but is built only in the company of those where love is a genderless given.

Tommy Madden's hand is held with the positivism of trust, and he is grateful, for of late his thumbs have felt awkward. A stocky man, adept when working in the mines, Tommy has been through paperwork and forms so that he can claim his benefits, then forced onto a Restart course where new skills involve typing at an alien computer.

"They've got me typing out bloody letters, forms, spreadsheets, and loads of things I can't remember. These bloody big paws keep hitting two keys, and I have to go back and start again. God Dickie, it's not for me. It's a torture, for sure. I've not got the patience for it. You know, I go back to where the mine was from time to time, look at the building that's coming up from hell, and I think to myself, why aren't we still down there? You know, there's still tons of coal down there, and I'm reading in the papers how Britain is importing coal from other countries. It doesn't make sense, does it? So, I just keep pounding away, messing up and starting again because I have no choice. If I quit, then my benefit stops."

"You'll crack it, Tommy, don't worry."

"Yeh, okay. Well, all the best. I'll see you down the club for the Christmas party, I'm sure."

The social club was packed on Christmas Eve with lustrous palms engaged on entrance, wishing well for futures remembered from every last year. They did not rest once seated, but were vigorously renewed at mingling, each recognition beaming, rising to greet; an alimentative coalescing of spirits, energised amongst a microcosm of the town. Through the hours, it was easy for all to forget hardships and worries and just indulge, singing along to the band's seasonal covers, locked into uncoordinated rounds of drinks, sealed off from number-crunching, form-filling, decimal-point worlds. This was an autonomous state, with no fear of scratches on backs billing for repayment. A manifesto of idle and ideological banter was worked out in gulps and intermittent pissing, in intakes and exchanges, joyously propositioned on common ground. Empathy and sympathy and droopy-eyed optimism procreated amongst the scattered tables and chairs, pricking the loosened limbs to disperse impulsively, taking their recollections of the evening and night to parasympathetic streets and satellite areas of town.

For the morning, dulled minds were not taken by religion to worship for a God or son a god or any motherfucking god. There was no need for synthetic cleansing, or laughable praying; the head-banging, skull-fucking tedium reading out the riot of things to regret and reasons to be meek. Better still to wake up, like Gary Orton and Lisa Burnham, and watch gleefully as Anthony offers "Father Kiss-mass" and opens the easily ripped paper bought from Dickie Chadwick's stall to fall into the imagined kingdom of a new toy, involved in its workings and possibilities and forsaking the other parcels. In George Lewis' house, an exchange of gifts is peripheral to the love exchanged in preparation for seeing their grandchildren gathering amidst the warmth of a three-bar fire, hemmed in by decorations and wrappings and bowls of snacks and glasses. They would love and exchange and settle around the television, not watching as conversation drifted towards reverie, taking turns to be children with the nippers pushing plastic cars around pieced together roads and dressing dolls for voice-over innocence.

Even the likes of Natalie Maines, Jenny Byland and Stuart Adams, their cynicism and belligerence still kicking for direction, were soothed by the template of a past pulsing with the cataclysmic joy of childhood not long gone. A reticular formation joined them unknowingly on living room floors, ripping open surprises to keep them young.

Slumping after dinners, the ritual of ignoring the Queen and the Commonwealth; just some tarted-up woman wearing the costume we had chipped in to buy her, preaching peace and love from her ivory tower. With the tax we paid her, for cocking up her nose around the world, we could have had another hospital to care for the miners now wheezing.

"My family have had a lovely Christmas in our palace, thanks to the overwhelming generosity of my people's taxes. It's been another busy year of shopping for clothes and visiting foreign countries, and although it is a demanding job, we do it for you, our loyal subjects. My husband has been able to indulge his hobby of racist banter around the world and find some time to study the cultural significance of Bernard Manning. God bless his quaint little stereotyping, he's such a blast at the dinner table. Charles has been busy too, cheating on his wife, using your money wisely on helicopter flights to the local off-license and dusting down the Royal train to cut ribbons. Diana's work for charity just shows how much she cares. She's not just a pretty face, you know. In between throwing herself down staircases, she still has found time to tell naughty dictators not to use landmines. I'm sure she'll get around to speaking to our government about not selling them in the first place.

Of course, this is the time of the year when thoughts turn to the true meaning of Christmas, and how we must take some time to think about the suffering around the world. I do hope next year someone makes a bit more effort to feed the starving and enable the poor of the world to be immunised against diseases. I'm sure someone will. Well, let's hope so. It does make one feel guilty, having all these cars and accessories, but I know that my country understands that we only use what we need to. Anyway, have a good Christmas, because we don't really care as long as you keep giving us your money."

Whatever she says, the Queen mocks tragedy and suffering, laughing in the face of people like Ray and Mary Young, more eager to get through the day without crying as they reminisce about John fighting then dying for Queen and country. They tread a fine line, indulging reminiscences which keep alive the son who once played at the centre of their universe, pushing an Action Man through wrapping paper to fight injustice and evil; careful not to dwell on the space at their feet. In ellipses they move closer to each other and embrace to squeeze out the negatives, fragile in a loneliness that is not ignored by others.

Throughout the day, doors on Manic Street scrape and bark, shuffling open for an entrance, a handshake, a hug and an "all the best" over drinks. Casual invites are offered and accepted, the busyness of hours not standing still. The fluidity of movement keeps all within arm's length on the curving spine of Manic Street, lives intermingling without boundaries, kisses chinking over glass cheers until they are too tired to be alone.

New Year resolutions are broken before the decorations are removed and all the manic streets in town are skeletal once more, revealing bony structures awaiting the condemnation of another year without government.

The sea front is a parade of weariness with closed buildings festering intent amidst the muscular determination of those arcades and parlours straining to breathe. A line of facades looks out to the ocean with the wisdom of gravestones, preaching in sleep about an atrophying past. At the top end, the grey structure of a closed garage, then a boarded-up teashop, and the small time arcade that didn't keep up with fashions, before a cell of life in the lifeboat headquarters. The back end of an old supermarket shows its arse to the waves, long since bought out by cheaper retail where everything is ephemeral. Closer to the centre, as if in retreat, are some places still open, huddled together, and reliant on each other. Three arcades, a pub, two chip shops and an ice cream parlour are flaking along the pockmarked row, their nerves frayed by the interspersed plywood canvasses. Upon these, undying love is still noted, but there is also amorphous hate, sprayed and carved: an autopsy for blame. *Pakis out* and *NF* are tattooed in with penknife and biro, from right-handed, wrong-headed imbeciles transplanting their disaffection.

Bill Harris took some paint from his shed and obliterated the image, but up close to closure, you could still run a finger along the letters and feel the hostility.

The sea front was a place for youths to congregate, to hang around and waste the time they were unskilled to utilise. When they had fed the machines that teased them with regurgitations, spent up on the thrills of video games and necessity of chips, they had only the suffocating communication, built on their prick-bruised experiences, to fill judgmental waking. An invisible government could not be blamed for their predicament, so their lashing tongues found unity in obscenity and racism; a common enemy of difference.

Stuart Adams, strengthened by his iconoclasm, fashioned his garments upon literary rebellion, piercing his eyebrow as a statement of insurrection. He only had Natalie and Jenny, but in their own minds they were a formidable army, intellectually potent and knowingly pissing off those abandoned to ordinariness and the drudgery of gender stereotypes. They frequently celebrated being outsiders during hours spent at their cave, and when they walked about town to howls of derision, they were quick with a put down, expeditious in escape.

Moving home alone one evening, Stu was caught between the departure of his companions and the safety of home, by a gang of four lads shouting out insults.

"You fucking puff! Do you wanna suck my cock, then?"

"Which one? Is it the one in your trousers, or the one on your head?"

Stu was running before they could process the wit that would decapitate them were they not so intellectually short. But the streets were deserted, silent buildings no longer offering the sanctuary of life within. He was chased and tripped at the end of Manic Street, in the garden of a smashed up home. They punched and kicked, unstitching his skin with ballot paper crosses, marking his distinction with fascistic violence, leaving cuts and bruises like stars, before me and Mikey chased off the gang.

"Fucking ignorant cunts!" he cried as he twisted in agony, blubbering uncontrollably for the shattering of a world he had created for himself. We helped him up and took him home, passing on to his mother and father a different son, shorn of escapism, as vulnerable again as the one in the ageing photographs hung around the living room.

Such violence was becoming more of a feature around town with certain areas riddled with petty crime and drug addiction, and now spoken of by turns excitably and lamentably as no-go places. In contrast, a shiny new D.I.Y. store was opened where the pit used to dominate. A Tory politician was present to open it and offer "this marks another phase in this town's regeneration with the jobs created having a knock on effect for the area."

"Why don't you fuck off back to London where the rest of the Tory scum are?" came from amid a meagre crowd, belched from its belly, preceding one beautifully flighted egg, which splattered on the speaker's suit. It prompted laughter and cheers before the police made an arrest despite hostile booing.

There was employment to be had there. Dickie Chadwick, Tommy Madden and George Lewis were all told they had to take the jobs on offer or they would lose benefits. In truth, they were glad to be working, whatever the job, even if it meant starting on a low salary, on short term contracts without redundancy packages and with an imperative to learn new skills before they could secure any improvements in conditions.

George says, "It's simple enough work, unloading, stacking, and pushing a trolley. It's nice to have something to get up for, to work up a sweat again, and to earn from your toil. I shouldn't really have any nostalgia for pit work, or reckon that what I'm doing now is somehow less worthy than that, but I do."

"I know what you mean," replies Bill Harris. "It's because we had a sense of working for our own community down the pit, that somehow what we did kept things together. Maybe it did, but we shouldn't be under any illusion that we weren't also cheap labour for governments making plenty of money from our toil."

"I'm glad there's Dickie and Tommy at the new store, but we don't work side by side. There's always something else to do, no time for banter. Lads half my age are telling me this or that needs doing urgently, so we only have the breaks to chat.

Y'know, as dirty and dangerous as the pit was, there was a sense of pride amongst us. There was nobility in somehow being a part of a long history, doing what your father did. Now, most of the people we work with seem to be just passing through. There's no pride to be had in replenishing what has been sold, no sense of producing something important. Most of them that come in are from out of town. I always thought D.I.Y. was a practical thing, not something you did for pleasure. I don't get it."

"It's interaction with materialism rather than people. I suppose it's what this society's about now, post-Thatcher. You know George, we're out of date."

"And this town is our museum. They'll be bussing people in to gawk before long. I'd better get my flat cap out."

They chuckled, moved on by the invisible commerce police, rolling their frames down Manic Street's aisle, home for antiquated suppers. The dateless stimulation of Being had settled at a point in most lives where the new was not sought, but dismissed with a passivity tired out by defeat. Vital sparks smoked up puffs in idle congregations, revisiting former glories, or else preaching to the open spaces about affairs in semantically separate places.

Danny Madison, itching for an election when he would be Labour's candidate, was feverish in preaching, "We've got to make a stand against the far right who are trying to shame our town, peddling their racism to the vulnerable and disenfranchised. Their ideology patronises us, wanting us to stand still with hate. Don't believe them when they spout lies about immigrants taking jobs. We know it is the carelessness of Tory policy that has tried to destroy this area. The far right is basically saying we are too stupid to see the bigger picture, so here is an easy target for blame. They can tart up their image all they like, but they are no more than vile Nazis." A smattering of applause amongst the thirty or so Labour and anti-fascist activists gathered at the library annex. "I want this community reborn through social changes that will once again put the needs of the many at the centre of policies. We have fortitude, an intellect rich with history and experience, and we have always been aware that there is strength in togetherness with no barriers of race or religion. Mohammed Khan had his shop daubed with racist graffiti last week, by some mindless thugs intent on driving him out. Since the early eighties, Tory policy seems to have been a concerted attempt to force people to leave this town, and now that job has been passed over to racist idiots. We can't be complacent, which is why over the next few months, as this discredited government takes the last crumbs for the public plate, we must be out there telling traditional Labour supporters what we stand for and what we oppose."

Danny distributed leaflets in packs of fifty, each one bullet-pointing the idiocy and dangers of far right thinking, to be spread around the pores of town, pricking consciences and trying to connect to tragedies that are being enacted amongst the dust of television news reports. Slipping between sensation, the acupuncture of cattle prods and electrical torture, dribbling onto the world stage from last year's thing. Something about half a million Tutsis murdered by Hutus in Rwanda, about an inelegant genocide of barely clothed races: Something too complex to make the headlines when Princess Diana was parading.

For every person like Danny, articulating warnings about "Tutsi revenge," there were others wrapped up in how "*Eastenders* will end."

Blood splashes in other continents didn't make front-page splashes on tabloid front pages more concerned with the circulation of celebrity.

"When Richey James went missing, Richey Edwards found solace, I'm sure," said Jenny in the smoking cave. "I hate the way it's being presented in glorified terms by the press. They're so excited by the enigma, it's like they are willing it to be so special. They love the burn out and fade away glow of rock star excess, but his disappearance is nothing like that. It's sad and ordinary."

"He struck me as someone despairing at the way greater tragedies were ignored," said Stu. "He would have hated the press' poring over his life when they should be concentrating on genocide in Europe."

"But, unless he reappears, he's stuck in rock history now, ready to be reeled out with Kurt Cobain, Ian Curtis, Jimi Hendrix," added Natalie. "In *Les Mouches*, Jean-Paul Sartre said human life begins on the far side of despair. Richey's life seemed to be about his difficulty in leaving behind innocence, like he never could lift himself beyond the far side of despair."

"One thing that sticks in my mind, that I read somewhere," began Stu, "is that he said you don't make any true friends beyond the age of seventeen. I find that quite beautiful."

"What about us, though?" asked Natalie. "We stopped at thirteen, didn't we?"

The smoking cave appealed to all three because of its Bohemian atmosphere, created by strange, surreal wall drawings and markings and gut-ripped daubing. Most were their own design, but some had already been committed before they made the cave their own, by unidentified beings either dead, departed or disinclined to return. Natalie, Jenny and Stuart were there to "punk dialogue to fuck," as they'd dubbed it:

"Come on, punk dialogue to fuck, you start off Stu."

"I've been thinking about disappearance. Abortions are disappearance."

"Smoking is disappearance," said Natalie upon a drag.

"If only the Pope's mother had gone for a back street abortion, do you think his spirit would be up there in heaven rapping with God?"

Jenny looked at the cave art. "These drawings don't seem to disappear. We are all going to disappear though. We don't really mean anything do we? So we might as well disappear."

"How come we always end up in some existentialist wet dream?" asked Stu. "Why do we think misery has so much virtue? Is it any more real than a three minute pop song about love?"

Natalie had some preaching to do: "Which is why your music collection is all Nick Cave, Joy Division, The Clash, etcetera etcetera. If you want to play the devil, punk boy, clean your skin and get some proper clothes. The reason we end up here so quickly is for the comfort of suffering, the sensation of undiluted anger. It makes us real, and even if that's only what we believe, at least it separates us from all the others at school who thinking Oasis are touched by genius. Or think that even the real

Beatles mean anything. I was born the day Lennon died and that's been a fuckin' good swap for planet Earth, so puke out your rhetoric Stu!"

"Punk dialogue to fuck, Natalie!" celebrated Jenny.

"Yeh, yeh," said Stu with the humour of resignation. "Punk is dead. We won't be school kids this time next year. I've hated the place more than most, but there will be something lost forever next summer. Yeh, they'll be college, but I feel loss at what's happening. Innocence was taken for granted, and now it's gone, or maybe going."

Jenny replied, "I can't wait to leave. Can't wait to leave this scruffy town and all the small minds that cram into its routine without questioning anything. These small minds meet small minds and breed small minds, further diluted. One day, a rain is gonna come and wash them all away."

7
JUNKED ON DECEIT

When the sun came out, the sea front took faltering steps backwards, beckoning sunbathers to sleep under blue skies, and rousing kids with monetary chatter cranking arms and pressing buttons that would send out missiles. The great British seaside picture was being approximated at other European resorts, released by climates to idle contemplation of what might possibly be better.

The preachers were there too, browned on amnesia, with elders positioned at the centre of children building empires in the sand. This safe haven of merriment gassed themselves into melting slumber, blissfully surrounded by the sounds and icons which were as durable as cliché. Lisa and Gary popped out a castle for Anthony, clawing into a mound, encouraging him to pile the sand back into the red plastic vessel and clap excitedly at his own creation.

Sky blue uniforms with spunked-up guns patrolled the enclave under the auspices of rudely financed democracy. The delicacies of argument, the buffet of reason, were frittering away time in arguments and objectives, drawing up a plan to stay on the fence. Warplanes overhead blocked out the sun, causing the sunbathers to switch positions for pure reception. The barbarians were free to march in, only molested by carefully chosen language from those with cleansed hands.

John Major, apparently the British Prime Minister, spoke of the need to "maximise the political pressure," as Dutch peacekeepers daubed silent obscenities whilst the vulnerable cowered. In the chamber of despair, the artistry of cocks ejaculating over women: playful humiliation chalked into walls. Men and boys are separated from the fingers of families and trucked out to the blind spots of European brotherhood. The wailing bewilderment of women does not travel to places where bodies are riddled with disbelief, choked on questions, which will go unanswered by fattened democracies.

We are sunbathing all across the free world, anchored on deckchairs by the holocaust's conscience. Lisa Burnham, once discoloured by snapshots like the Dutch soldiers' Neanderthal drawings, would lose Gary and Anthony to be cleansed by the ocean, shrieking with the other women as love drowned amongst the waves. George Harris and his band would be taken to schools and playing fields and shot in the head, then scraped into graves and covered in bloodied red tape.

We do nothing, but sun ourselves with the vaguely optimistic ruminations about how we might escape our own prosaic little tragedies. We have not organised our guilt into action, but instead are merely satiated by the ceremony of sympathy, wrung out from a safe distance.

As shadows move in and we kick the sand from our shoes, our leaders put a squeeze on irony with a Rapid Reaction Force, sending in the armoury to explode a red carpet for celebratory march. No cheers from the widows and orphans of the eight thousand slaughtered.

"We let it happen," Danny Madison said, "and history will judge our complicity with a clarity we are now too complacent to grasp. I see John Major and Bill Clinton boldly talking about saving lives, defeating evil, showing how the world community can intervene to make a positive difference, but there's little said about Srebrenica. It doesn't sit well with the triumphal speeches. You've got to wonder how quick to intervene the western world would have been if there was an oil rich country in turmoil."

Danny stopped himself, truncated with an impending apology to Ray Young. "So..."

"It's alright, don't patronise me Danny. The Gulf War was all about oil. I know that now. John knew that in the end. Soldiers are the pawns of politicians these days. It's easy for people like Major to send young men and women to their deaths, because the world is too used to such conflicts to really care beyond the initial sense of sadness. There's no annual commemoration of those that died in the Gulf, no elegant speeches about the bravery of those fighting a noble cause. Bloody hell Danny, Saddam Hussein is still there, still the same tyrant as before. And what are we doing now to reduce this evil dictator? We're using sanctions to kill tens of thousands of civilians, most of them children. What is their tyranny? These people are victims and we neglect them like we neglected the people of Srebrenica."

"We don't stop being active though, just because our leaders are imbued with the apathy of contentment," added Bill Harris, opening a pulpit on Manic Street. "They haven't knocked down this street yet."

Raging against the dying light of summer, a cause was to be found much closer to home when Liverpool Dockers were sacked because of grievances about not working overtime for a disputed rate. All 329 men from Mersey Docks and Harbour mounted a picket line and they too were sacked.

"Mersey Docks and Harbour have been fattened by government funding. This year they'll make over thirty-one million in profits," announced Bill Harris at a meeting to organise support. "Shame on the company, who have been so quick to sack the men whose toil made that profit. Shame on Trevor Furlong too, the managing director: a man who took an eighty-seven thousand pounds pay rise recently. You know, it now brings his earnings to three hundred and sixteen thousand pounds a year, not including a share option of two hundred and ninety three thousand pounds. The facts are there, if you want to look. It's typical of management that they should judge this as a side issue as they hungrily seek to devour more profits at the expense of workers. Comrades, right now there are meetings like this all around the country, and indeed the world, seeking to gather support and raise money for the Dockers. We live in a cynical age, where the Right have managed to demonise union power, driving it to extinction because workers rights somehow get in the way of making more and more money. We must make this stand, right now, like it's our last stand, and keep fighting until this government finally topples."

Former pit workers cheered, sensing a chance to hit back after previous defeats, raised again like a punch-drunk boxer.

Dickie Chadwick inspired a secretive collection at the D.I.Y. store, and got a verbal warning for his troubles. He, George, Pete and Ray put on a few gigs to raise money at the social club. Their wives – Helen, Rachel, Mary along with Mandy Chadwick, Katherine Harris and Joan Madden – were the most aggressive, the organisational skills acquired during the Miners' Strike put to good use in arranging jumble sales and coffee mornings.

In the winter, I published my book of photographs, setting aside some of the money from sales for the Dockers' fund. I called the book, *Ghosts of the Working Age*, and to my surprise it got some publicity in the region, and there I was, clumsily preaching on local television:

"It's meant to be a celebration of life in my home town, but also a reminder of what is being lost in the name of progress. Of course, such progress, whatever it really means when livelihoods and communities are destroyed, is an unstoppable force, so the book is also a chance to record images that are disappearing. I didn't want it to be a sepia-tinged fairytale of working class life. Those kinds of books are nice and harmless, and they have their place, but they tend to direct attention away from the bigger picture. Some of the images in this book are deliberately raw, showing suffering and despair as my attempt to make those in government actually take note of what their policies actually do to people. I think we've had sixteen years where Tory governments have only measured progress by finances and the artifice of commerce. We live in a society now where materialism and individuality hold sway rather than the health and fluidity of communities. Yes, it's an old idea called Socialism, which now seems to be a dirty word, but the core values are those that most people believe in, I'm sure of that."

Dad was so proud and he became a kind of secretary, dealing with printers and wholesalers and spluttering to the post office to send off orders. I believed it sustained him as he battled against cancer, doing inventories in his hospital bed as he determined to make it through the winter.

Varicose street theatre progressed through its usual carnival of expectation weighed against the frozen reality of situations unchanged, or else snapping bones within the body of superficial contentment. Frost elbowed its presence upon skin-paving, left progress as unsteady as naive honesty brutalised by state-sponsored lies. We were humble and meek, raging fires inside to keep us warm, opening old wounds to feed the need of emotion, scattering tracks of blood to salt passions ingrained in the template of our class: the absolute design of perfection from embryo to invisible abuse.

8
LIBRARIES GAVE US POWER

That Christmas, Lisa Burnham announced she was pregnant, and began making marriage plans with Gary Orton for reasons ignorant of dogma. They said "I've never been happier," to neighbours who knew such words had stripped the bones from contagious cliché.

"I knew Gary would be a great dad," said Brenda Maines, "and she's got herself straightened out an' all."

"I've seen the mother around there the other day," added Liz Byland. "Looks like she's sorted herself out 'an all. It's nice to have your family round at Christmas."

"That's what it's all about."

In and out of the houses left occupied on Manic Street, connections were shook through the cold, welcoming in the anarchy of senescent comforts too much raging against the light to know their place. Time passes through the bricks and mortar like occasional rushes of attic-bound adolescence, unplucking the hoarse Sellotape of cardboard boxes and sorting through the jingles that have made it through the year. We join hands for Auld Lang Sine and wake as goose bumps on climactic mornings.

Susie Pilgrim had returned to England, telephoning from London, eager for me to travel to the capital, where she was now writing for a marginal magazine, fervent to take my book around the connections she had made. I longed to set a date, but could make only vague promises due to Dad growing more fragile.

Hearing Susie's voice reminded me of the past, of a perspiration of love and the eeriness of mortality. Although the season was abundant with familiar reassurances, this Christmas was imbued with sadness; a time when I barely left the home on Manic Street as I ruminated around its confines and stubbed out memories in the back garden.

The book was successful enough for me to contemplate moving out and, at the blood-rush point of finally finding some tenuous direction for my twenty-five years, I was indulgent in the anarchy of snapshots that had brought me to this point. It wasn't difficult to recall myself as young and wide-eyed and surrounded by the family embodying all history and possibility. Whenever we visited grandparents, the rooms of their house always had a sense of the past, beyond the archaism of a pantry and a coal fire. Even the walls and ceilings, though clean and well cared for, breathed silently the fashions of bygone construction. I could vividly picture the tiles in the bathroom, gleaming despite ageing, the elaborate toilet chain readied for religious absolution, and the smooth and rounded ceramics with no time for the square fascism of the new. Now, this sense was prevalent in my own home, nudging me to conclusions amputating the present. So, I dwelled on the notches of incidents and experiences and caught myself isolated when father was sleeping. Here was where brightness once beamed in nondescript routines, over breakfast and dinner and slumped on a sofa full of others.

The dishevelled back garden, where we once tried out the day's new presents, was now barely used but for infrequent upkeep. Here was where Mikey and me kicked a ball and screamed at dispossession by the enormous figure still in his clod-hopping boots, shaking of the dust of the pit as he turned us inside out. Back then a sky high ball over fence just required jumping over two low level planks to the neighbours' gardens, but even when the vogue of being penned in by high panel-fencing meant running around the front to knock on a door, there was a shared glee which asked "who's winning, Pete?" before the ball was retrieved.

Through the stubbornness of winter, Mikey was up every weekend; there to alleviate not only Dad's pain, but also the loneliness he knew I was feeling. When Dad slept, we kicked small talk about in search of the vein of emotion:

"England are looking good for the Euro Championship, don't you think?" he asked me.

"Yeh, if Gascoigne's fit. It doesn't seem like five minutes since we were all watching Italia Ninety. It still hurts when they show clips of the semi-final defeat."

"Dad always said Venables was the man to do it."

"He'll be getting the wall chart out again, no doubt." I paused, swelled with uncertainty. "Jesus, Mikey, I don't think he's going to make it through."

He held me as I cried, wrapped around me an accumulation of images from a time stood-still. He was my big brother again, offering irresistible warmth like the optimism of his once pure ambitions. I was the sound of ageing machines, creaking and leaking into the shared oxygen of Manic Street: the rag and bones of ingrained bonds wheeling around streets in search of artefacts to connect with the past. I bawled to nulliparous futures, no longer able to beat blood to a way of life suffocating on mere nostalgia.

"I feel so alone, Mikey. People come round to see Dad all the time, and when I look at them – at George, Bill, Ray – I see how old they have grown, and it shocks me; scares me even to think of how time will roll them over and out. I just see myself in this town, alone for ever, too scared to face change. It's pathetic, but I so want to be a child again and have all that was going on around me to be alive again."

"You've got everything to look forward to Pete, with your book, your ideas. You're creativity has no boundaries. You can leave this town easily and be a success, I have no doubt."

"But, I have such a connection to this place, I feel even more desperate when I imagine leaving it all behind. It's like I'll no longer be able to be a part of my memories, like I'll be so far away from all the experiences that I'll be empty."

"It's a wrench, but after the pit closed, Mum and Dad always wanted us to get out, you know that. We can't cling to the past, but it'll always be a part of us. I haven't forgotten all the times we've shared when we were young, and you won't either. And Petey, I'll always be here for you, man."

This was the brother who'd enthralled me around the dinner table, sweeping gestures mapping out his golden dreams in a pocket of resistance before his imprisonment. He overstayed for days and lost money miles away. We toiled at nature and gorged out memories, fuelling glial cells in preparation for departure.

Dad died with spoken love a fever on his lips, preaching the unity of generations immune to the surgery of fashions.

The funeral drew familiar faces, leaving imprints in a thin layer of snow. I did not cry through the service and, although we were spastic inside stained glass, I felt words beyond religion.

Dad had divided the house, but Mikey said it was mine for as long as I needed it. He stayed with me for a week, helping me to clear out clothes and inconsequential clutter, sharing out mementoes to disappear inside cardboard.

During the impotent labour of grieving, Susie telephoned, crying when I told her and in pain to visit. I knew when Mikey was leaving, and I didn't want to be alone, so I asked her to come up to fill the void.

This was love, a re-connection with the frivolous days spent evaporating ideas around the town's secret pores; matured by experiences which threw us about inner and outer space. We dined on the living room floor, touching the receptors of innocence, laughing at our once muscular promise and eager to breathe each other's present.

"...Hanging around the arcades, with our adolescent philosophies, thinking we would change the world."

"But only when we had no more money to play the slot machines," I added.

Susie laughed, shuffled close to me as we lay out against the foot of the sofa. "This town has really changed, Pete. You've got all these new retail outlets, selling bargain basement stock, and D.I.Y. stores and grubby fast food places. They all should be new and shiny, but they already have a tacky, decayed look about them. Then you go around town, and the state is shocking. I mean, just rows of empty, boarded up houses and streets waiting for demolition. Where have all the people gone?"

"Moved away, or passed away. This street's the same. We've been fighting to keep it, but for the last few years Marcus Bowles has been trying to get it knocked down so he can build new places. They say it'll be affordable housing, but Danny Madison's seen the plans and most of the area is going to be for expensive ocean-view flats."

"Will it happen?"

"Well, it hasn't so far, but y'know, some people – and you can't blame them – have taken the money and left. It seems pretty inevitable. They say that compulsory purchase orders are next."

"What are you going to do with this place?"

"I don't know. There's nothing much left for me here."

"Come to London, Pete. You can stay with me, and the magazine I work for is always looking for photographers and writers with new ideas."

"Thanks, Susie. It might be something I have to do, but I'm not ready yet. I think I want to stay around here for a while. I couldn't give you a good reason. Keeping this street from Marcus Bowles is maybe the reason, you know, one last fight against The Man."

"Okay, well it's an open offer. By the way, I'm going to Liverpool next week to talk to the striking Dockers. Why don't we meet up? Bring your camera; we might get something together for the magazine."

"Yeh, I'd like that."

Separation made our love exhilarating, impetuous, and invulnerable in its carelessness. We spent the next few days rattling around our old spots, running sore on laughter of reminiscences, and then retreating indoors to indulge wine-filled fantasies of overthrowing the government. Immeasurable passion left us naked until weary afternoons, touching sensitivities as the world creaked through a routine outside.

When I'd waved her away and returned inside, it was the first time I'd been alone in the house for months, and I cried in confusion and loneliness, then clawed through the days before we met up again.

The striking Dockers were a hearty and determined group of men and women fighting for their jobs. I took photographs of them with their banners and placards, merrily smiling for the camera like I was some relative at a ceremony. We went to some houses for shots with families and I tried to capture their lack of pretension; that these were the people all over Britain being cut loose and left to die by the need for profits. These images were basic, because what really mattered were their words, which reminded me of the preachers on Manic Street, alive with logical anger when the miners were striking. They had the dignity of reason, articulating grievances with an optimistic innocence, believing that anyone with humanity must surely agree with the injustice of their predicament.

"They've been trying to destroy us for a few years, looking for an excuse to sack us and employ casual labour. So, we had to work longer hours with increased workloads. Basically, you do the twelve hour shift or you're sacked."

"Then they started to place us on call on our days off. You'd be at home with your family and you'd get a call saying you had to get back to work 'cos shifts had been changed. And if they couldn't get you over the phone, you'd get a hand delivered message to get back to work. Once, I'd only been home for five hours and I was ordered back. A friend of mine got disciplined for not answering his phone when he was off."

"Thing is, we always felt we'd fought for these jobs and we went back to work because we'd didn't want to give them an excuse to get rid of the jobs."

"They had these new contracts, said all the existing jobs were going and new jobs were being created to fit in with a new system. And of course, the new system is just trying to fuck us some more. So, we refuse and they sack us. Some of us have been here all our lives, and now what? Re-train at fifty-five years of age? We've got to fight, there's nothing else. The Tories have screwed working people for too long, but they were powerful then. Now, they are so weak it's pathetic. The Unions and the Labour Party can actually win this fight if they want to."

If they wanted to, they could. But the 'If' was wracked with the anxiety of previous election failures and could not countenance being aligned to anything vaguely associated with Socialism. The Dockers, for all their spirit, optimism and determination were not so much being sold down the river by Tory government, as by those they thought represented their cause. It resonated back to Manic Street, with preachers such as Bill Harris alive to the uncoiling betrayal:

"We are an anachronism, George, that's for sure. This way of life, based on social responsibility and morality, is dead. You know, even after the pit closed and Thatcher and Major continued to buy off the popular vote with tax cuts, I still thought that there was a voice of reason out there; that they were many, many like us who thought that union strength and sharing the wealth could help create a more just and contented society. I still thought that once the Labour Party had reorganised that it would be committed to Socialist ideals. But God, I must have been blind. It's a different world now, where no one wants to rock the boat, more than happy instead to edge towards the middle ground: in politics, in humanity, in diluted intellects. You'll get mocked nowadays for talking about raising taxes to improve schools and hospitals. It's all, don't kick up a fuss, and just keep Middle England happy."

The Dockers have been shit on from a great height. The TGWU, supposedly there to represent them, has cut them loose. Bill Morris, General Secretary, goes up to Liverpool with a shit sack of empty rhetoric:

"I am proud to be with you," Morris says. "There can be no turning back and no backsliding until victory is won."

Working class cheers are so easily roused. We have been stupid so long now, it's taken for granted. Morris won't even recognise the dispute as a strike. He's an empty bullshitter, locked in velvet halls preening for a knighthood.

"Tony Blair won't get involved either, will he? He doesn't want to scare away any potential voters. That's all his thinking is about"

"There are plenty of Socialists still left in the party, George," interrupted Danny. "We'll fight from within. He can't take away the soul of the party."

"And, you know, we're all willing for the next government to be Labour. We'll vote for Blair to get rid of the Tories, but you can't help feeling he hasn't got the guts to question capitalist ideology. More than that, I think he actually believes in it." Bill Harris widened his hands. "Working hands, these. Labour voting hands. They are rough to touch, thickened with subservience to what was once a common good. They have spent a lifetime fingering for crumbs. Now all they are wanted for is empty applause and the simplicity of a cross. They are cumbersome when trying to find shape in materialism, fidgeting for a conclusion to the experiences and intellect worked at for a sense of participation. Obsolete, they now dig make-believe graves for credibility. I'll see you down below."

Bill walked off to retire from the fever of preaching, to meander around his daily routine, passing the small talk of generations.

Natalie, Jenny and Stu were positioned on their scarred bench, working through school-imposed texts, dipping into the luxury of library books to corroborate and expand the ideas they were igniting.

They greeted Bill, momentarily static in responses, before returning to revision. For them, the confines of the classroom were a mere annoyance as they hungrily took the basics of lessons to nourish their knowledge.

Notices pinned on cobwebs informed that they could purchase the books for pennies, as the library would be closing next month.

"Where are we supposed to go to get the books we want?" demanded Natalie.

"They're cutting back, expanding the main library in town. You'll have to go there," said the librarian. "It's a shame, but there's nothing we can do."

"Starve us of knowledge, that's what they are trying to do. Keep us dumb and malleable, that's what it's really about," said Stu.

The glorious weekenders, on Friday and Saturday night binges, would be baffled by why space in their soaked brains might need to be filled with the implications of closure. For them, patriotic in inebriation, there was the joy of a new club and the generosity of time-untroubled happy hours. The lads and ladettes of Britpop, were busy with the glamour of recklessness, promiscuously apathetic to poverty; moneyed-up working classes following the herd, yobbish with language, indulging fantasies made up in lyrics where "fuck you!" was a manifesto. A design for life was good enough for them, no questions asked.

"Whatever life makes me, I don't care, 'cos I got this bottle and 'am gonna' get wrecked. I'm free, you see. No one tells me what to do."

With Britpop at its height, the Manic Street Preachers returned to kick against the pricks with *A Design For Life*, a song sitting uneasily with the music of the time. Here was a song detailing working class struggle without chaotic anger, but with a poignancy that reverberated beyond the terms of the lyrics, evoking a sense of loss.

The lad culture that parasitically aligns itself to Britpop, is a million miles away from this, an expansive, spirited, poignant defiance. "Libraries gave us power/Then work came and made us free" rushes life into old, bloodied socialists excavating Manic Street, needing to be liberated every day by the reason inherent in their language. These people are armed with knowledge, gnawing the well-heeled society with pure argument, severing tendons to weaken the glorious gloss of veins gushing self-loathing in every pound shed for fashion and artificial change.

These preachers will always demand a say in society, wrecking idle temples and forcing pure perspectives that skin the instant gratification of self-satisfaction But in the last year of the Conservative government, after years of Thatcher and Major and fat cats getting richer, things like libraries have to be closed down because there is no profit in them, whilst working class occupations have been decimated and collective bargaining power diluted. Questioning is to be suffocated by the breeding of ignorance.

They closed down the library round here with little fuss and bother beyond the diluted cover story of unspectacular faces collective on the front of the local newspaper. A petition was accumulated, presented to councillors eager to shake hands in a snap shot and offer the hypocrisy of empathy. Nothing changed.

Regret filters through the gentle tone of the song's first two lines, almost a punch-drunk acceptance of things. "What price now for a shallow piece of dignity?" is equally poignant; as in this capitalist society, everything has a price, even human emotion.

And for your pound, you will get some second hand emotion, something manufactured and unreal; something shallow and unsatisfying because that's all that's left after everything's been sold off.

Acolytes of Marcus Bowles slithered along front paths to gas the occupants of Manic Street:

"We're offering a price way above the value of your home, which will give you and your family more than enough to re-locate to one of the homes in our brochure." Throw in your soul and a retainer on your limbs, and we'll fashion you with VCR and satellite television, and a parking space for your poverty.

"Why don't you fuck off," said Brenda Maines, "go on, get away from this door! I've lived in this house all my life and its riches are more than you could know."

"I'm as uninterested as I was last month and last year, so don't disgrace my door anymore," said George Lewis.

A firing squad a rejection was worked through yet again, but once more in this erosive cycle, there was enough persuasion tempting another to weaken the street. You couldn't blame Lisa and Gary, who'd always been striving to move away. Expectant with another child and occasionally tormented by the home's dispassionate past, Lisa was continually gasping at the air of a tomorrow where she could skin-shed and rebuild.

The yearning through years, a repetitive strain, felt like a trudge, like a Jarrow march for the bruised, battered and beaten: "I wish I had a bottle" and a desire to "wear the scars/To show from where I came" implicates working class life in a routine of violence, but for those cut adrift from working class sense of community and purpose, there is still a desire to wear the scar and identify with that life. If modern society is all about consumerism and branding, then the persona here seeks a branding more honest than the skin-sinking stamp of Nike or Gap. In this culture, puked haplessly on by the lad mag lifestyle of beer, tits and ironic celebration of all that is crass and shallow, there seems only one ambition: "We only want to get drunk." Perhaps this is even the working class, now moneyed up and eager for hedonism.

Marcus Bowles could afford cocaine, could get screwed without effort, drunk on investment and feeding off the disorientation of the class from where he came:

"Everything must go, it's just a question of time. Those empty houses will never be filled. Don't worry boys, have another beer. Next time we go around, we'll be telling them their homes are going to be condemned anyway. Compulsory purchase orders are licking their lips. It's not going to be healthy living on that street. Tell them prices will fall and before long they'll have to sell their homes for next to nothing. Everything must go!"

Miners and Dockers, Railwaymen and Doctors, all are removable if the price is right. Dignity and possibility can be amputated by profit, and you can wear a swastika sticker to say you've participated in the sale.

"I'd forgotten how good they were," I said to Susie after hearing the album *Everything Must Go*. It took us to our past amid the imperatives of the future. It's a political album of some subtlety whilst also eschewing the polemics of the earlier work (though, as later work would attest, this is not because the band felt that those polemics were any less vital). More tellingly for the band, now a three-piece without Richey, this is a watershed album: a throwing out of old baggage and preconceptions. "It should be uneven; some new lyrics and some Richey lyrics and the hesitant beginnings of a band readjusting, but it is their most accomplished work to date, thematically consistent and lyrically mature without being patronising or clichéd."

The mood of the album is one of loss, or at least something vital worn down and distorted. This is evident from the opening song, *Elvis Impersonator: Blackpool Pier* and its tale of a tacky performer with "Limited face paint and dyed black quiff/Overweight and out of date." It's a tawdry kitchen sink drama, juxtaposing an iconic American, and all the excess that he represents, with the potteries of Lancashire and cheap seaside entertainment. This, like the following *A Design For Life* is potency lost, and like the third track, *Kevin Carter*, Richey's staccato lyrics give it a spluttering, exhausted feel, the end of the pier show a metaphor for a life at the end of the line, or one numbly going through routines with little feeling or reason.

"Wasted your life in black and white", reverberates around the home I can barely cling to. The photographer exists as many things. He is the innocent seeking to capture moments from a life unravelling around him, to make the smiles wide by ordering their fixation. Click and whirring, approximations are frequently flashing light like an exploding star. From sofas to back gardens, from Christmas trees to monuments, from staging to stalking; the ugly is fascinating, the freakish is compelling. In this broken town, along this glass-strewn street, there lay symbols to pierce years of neglect.

He has to capture tragedy, has to make black and white of the horror, good and evil clicked but always prone to the ambiguity of those that perceive it. His conscience reminds him that history needs to be recorded, needs to be a lesson for future generations. But the damning click-click follows him into sleep, sounding like gravestones being chiselled as he circles above the crowd with hate-filled eyes.

He is touched by the horror, but appears insensitive. Am I like him, selling my book on struggles and strife? A feeling infects me that there is nothing left here to document, and that I must leave this town or atrophy with industry.

"Look," begins Bill, epitaphs clinging to gaps in his teeth, "you shouldn't stay here out of some notion of solidarity for your family or neighbours. Change is eating us, and some of it is for the better. There are no more opportunities for you here, but that's not your fault. These houses are going to be knocked down before too long, so get out while you can."

Those were the last words Bill ever said to me. On a sunny morning before most had awoke, he trundled to the beach and fell into the sand, clutching his heart where no one could see. He shivered for minutes, took headlamp flashes of his purpose and meaning, then shut out all progress fulfilled in the sand.

The funeral brought out every preacher who had ever had the spirit to ruminate and articulate. Faces from Old Labour's days of yore turned up to pay their respects without the chattering bugles of opportunity. Seventy-six years were inhaled in eulogies, each and every individual speaker sharing an equal sense of loss. Boyhood friends were jovial in picking out the impulses that had touched them in youth; from energetic child, running in circles with a gang, beating up paths on a paper round to save for a bike. Racing away from designation, they told how he read books for knowledge, dwelling on dictionary definitions for the tools to mould a future without control. Old miners scraped pictures of dedication to a cause, fighting small battles with the significance of justice.

"He always said to me," said George Lewis, "that the heart is left of centre in the chest. And he'd place his palm there and hand-beat a pause so we'd know each word he spoke, each action he engaged in, was born of that position. 'The heart nourishes brains, and is the foundations of reason' he said. 'And your politics should always come from there.' I've never met a more selfless man. We looked up to him because he was always so willing to argue for us, no matter how little or daunting the problem was. But more than that, he was our friend, and we shared many happy hours joking and laughing away trouble and strife. Our community has lost something in Bill Harris, but he has been such a presence that his memory and ideals will live long."

The sadness about was tangible but marginal. More prevalent was the resoluteness of spirit Bill's life had engendered, touching friends and colleagues. He was still there amongst the congregation and the crowds huddled outside the packed church, preparing spectral castigation for any who would be mawkish and maudlin.

His passing was acknowledged in local papers and the stuttering circulation of activist pamphlets, blown loose against the prevailing wind of celebrity chaos.

Bill Harris, remarkable and sincere, had no place in a culture more interested in an immediate fix of celebrity, where nostalgia replaces history so that all society boils down to is anecdotal masturbation. This is a culture unwilling to take responsibility, ignorant by choice: "Escape from our history," mocks the nouveaux riche zombies, taking their corpses to middle class aspirations. Drunken scum weekenders inebriated by the grunting chat-ups immaculate in fashion had no silences for Bill Harris. They had no interest in the history of tragedy and genocide, unless there was an open-fire sale of corpses. Humanity was for sale to fix up a thrill ride in the fast lane. Meaning had its price, keeping us quiet in the narcotic splendour of satellite dishes and the fashion accessories authenticated by star-fucking semen. Forget a history long out of womb; instead, salivate over designer labels parading in pop promos. It is the dismissal of history, of the knowledge that can go some way to explaining and answering deep questions. But in this society, the holocaust is reduced to a talking head gabbing about how *Schindler's List* was "the most powerful film in ages. It really hit home." Well, you know, *really* the holocaust itself wasn't so memorable. Not nearly as memorable as Blur versus Oasis for a coughing cash register of suffocated articulation.

For Katherine Harris, loneliness was a prompt, packing her belongings for departure to be closer to her grandchildren. She hated the thought of selling up, but Bill had often told her that she must move on once he had gone. So, there was apparent another numbness on Manic Street, another darkened spot not requiring a lampposts' repair. For the first time, there was regular talk of quitting the body:

"We're going to sell up and go," said Natalie, freezing on a bench, judging stringent cages, head cranked up from books with the shock of emotion. She neared tears. "But that doesn't mean I won't be meeting you both just as often as before."

"That's all my mam and dad are talking about these days," said Jenny. "The whole street is at the hangman's noose. Nah, Nat, we'll stay together."

"There is power in our union," added Stu with frostbitten irony. "Jesus, these animals look sad. Their vitality is all gone. It makes me feel so far away from home. Is this how we're all going to feel in the future?"

"Didn't we used to talk about getting away from home, leaving all the Neanderthals behind?" pondered Jenny.

"Yeh, and I still want to, but when you see all those people for Bill Harris' funeral, it makes you think about what they once had. Y'know, they're all old Socialists, and they've all been together for so long. I don't mean they've just lived there. They've actually lived their lives in and out of each other. And it's us too. We can all recall a childhood spent reckless with unmoulded comrades, before difference and enemies burned resentment into our perspective."

"I've never been name-called or chased by a Socialist," said Stu. "The weird thing is a lot of them old gadgies, you'd think they'd probably be quite conservative and hate people like us, but it's nothing like that. People like Bill Harris were against prejudice and intolerance. Y'know, you've got these working class union people, built like brick shit houses from a life of masculine labour, and they're against racism, homophobia, censorship, capitalism. They're fuckin' cool people really."

"Remember those times when we were sat around, dressed in black, made up like freaks, and Bill would come over and talk to us? He never said anything about getting a haircut or changing our clothes or getting a proper bloody job. He just wanted to fuckin' talk to us."

"Right then," said Jenny, "here's the pact: we will never drift apart, wherever we end up. We will always make time to get back to Manic Street and get back to out cave."

They placed their hands in a join at equal distance to their bodies and affirmed the bond, raising themselves to meander towards the zoo's exit.

"The superficiality of the show, from wild beast to pathetic ghost, withering away in the cage, these animals are symbolic of our hometown," concluded Stu. "From a roar to a grunt, all vitality has been dissipated by enclosure. These beasts once performed for thick, sweaty crowds stuffed with candy. Now they are impotent, shivering in manufactured dwellings. Jesus, this is depressing, let's not come here again unless we have a plan to set them all free."

The removals van, which loaded Mrs Harris' life, was small, unmarked by advertising, just a friend of a friend who could help out for cash in hand. Wives left standing and husbands aching to strain upright amid the boredom of inactivity and retirement waved her off. Some tears dried up in skin self-healing by design, but for the most part there was an airy benevolence about the amputation, busy at stitching before the wheels were in invisible revolutions.

Conscience had been sold, or else it would bind up in chains all those who had prickly feelings still circulating in their exhibitions. Conscience is no longer strength in this society, where the filth can have fun until the apocalypse, and even then they'll party at the end of the world party, so they can say they were there. Into this chaos, the second coming would go unnoticed. Conscience will not be required in the next millennium, so feed yourself on loathing, carve holes into your hands and crucify your compassion. When you're full from feeding yourself smiles, devour the misery that guilt always brings.

This is the voice seeking to shatter glass, muted by confinement, unable to spit out the madness. The junked-up body can take no more, each hit less original, more transitory.

I can't help feeling that I've lived this life as a ghost, that from the moment of birth, I have been merely passing through. And in this sea of inevitability, there are others – those that have never grown and whose innocence has been preserved in the memories of those that are also mere removables. We are unknown to each other, on a procession to our faker maker, solemnly bound by conscience as the hedonists and half-wits drink to a lower plain of erudition, shrieking in ignorance all around.

It's an agony of waking, an agony of waiting. For miles you can hear the ocean somewhere in the distance, somewhere more powerful than the sounds of the party: Waking to destiny, walking in line, lingering for a voice to stop this thing in full. I have been separate from Susie for too long. I have been rummaging around amid the bereavement of attic-anecdotes for too many drunken days. There is nothing more to photograph, no more words to write. I am at the full stop of my duration here, hanging on for an epilogue that demands distance and time for pyrrhic fruition.

"You could choose one of the homes from our relocation scheme," the programmed suit salivates to sell me.

"No, I'm just selling. You've got the soul; you've got the conscience, got every sinew of the dogged optimism once so alive on this street. Don't come barking for my dignity, please."

The befuddled trespasser had not been schooled on how to deal with subtlety of humanity, so he fidgeted with papers to present me: an aid to conclude his embarrassment.

I had so little to pack that preparation was accomplished in a day's worth of foolish regret. Time was to be spent on wistful farewells, sucking in the echoes of heartbeats to mark in my body from where I came. All that remained unpacked were a hi-fi and collection of compact discs, to play around with sounds crystallising my detouring moods. I was ready to go preposterously early, so that the indulgence of music and nostalgia would keep me narcotic for weeks more than days.

Removables is a song in keeping with the purgation that the Manic Street Preachers' album seeks, with a sense that the dominant internal symbols of the band's early years are being cast away. Underneath the albums' more glossy production values, its strings and orchestration, the sweeping expanses of songs like *A Design For Life* and *Australia*, there is the poignancy of loss, of change. In many ways, despite a collection of lyrics concerned with the fragility of presents, this album is perhaps the most evocative in terms of innocence lost. Pain is apparent in *Removables*, but also a need: "Aimless rut of my own perception/Numbly waiting for voices to tell me." We have here an acknowledgement of being caught in self-analysis, to the extent that only numbness now prevails. That this is Richey's song adds to the sense of purgation, knowing too that he had reached a dead end. The song's significance is accentuated by the uplift of the following track, *Australia*, its geographical sense seeming to suggest an escape, to a place as far away as possible. For me, London was the destination, but the expanse of the song spoke about the potency of anywhere in impending futures.

This is a song of cleansing. From the moment the guitars and drums wash in, there's a "praying for the wave to come now," a sense of regeneration in the image of drowning and cleaning. Being washed away is the past, an accumulated rut of routines clotting, entangled by unenlightening introspection. This I felt most strongly, caught between times, whittling away the bones of a life that was packed up, yet still looming and living in the structure of home. Instead of confinement and solitary musing, there is a desire to "fly and run till it hurts." *Australia* is an escape; a place where there is an interval to heal choking breath, where there can be found a peaceful sleep and no need to speak any words. The music carries the listener, transports effortlessly whereas the previous song was a solemn removing.

The final three tracks now play with movement, with a sense of peace, resulting in an ability to move into makeshift worlds with a degree of detachment not before experienced. *Interiors (Song For Willem De Kooning)* takes a third person view, resisting lyrical personalisation and the suffering that would once have brought.

Further Away is an apt title and marks another drift into the distance, experiences becoming ever more vague. This song presents the paradox of love and loss, that to feel so much emotion only makes absence and change all the more traumatic. The group, bonded since their youth, are changing, their sloganeering undergoing metamorphosis to something equally as passionate but profoundly more articulate. This song is a last look back at innocence, at childhood, at a time when things seemed to be more pure. Subsequently, it is a last indulgence of that regret and disappointment with adulthood: "The draining away just like an old man's dream." The imagery of draining away is again a cleansing motif, because innocence can be a burden when the purity of dreams is dissipated by the reality of cynicism. "The circular landscape comes back only with regret" suggests the routine and the inherent pressure to conform that have been a feature of the group's songs from the very beginning. We get the sense of coming full circle but finding no epiphany, no reconciliation. Here, the reference to "landscape" contrasts starkly with the imprisoned despair and industrial settings of the early songs. This is a song about at least searching for new meanings, and by doing so escaping the old destructive cycles. It is most poignant as it evokes a sense of threads being cut; a link back to Richey; that the more he is dwelt on – by his friends, but most significantly by fans and the media – the less real he becomes as a person, the more what he was becomes distorted.

Childhood - a pastoral memory - is slipping away, drifting with the clouds, fading into the distance. Here's where the kicking industry of back garden play leaked into the whole of the street and the oddness of teams not divided by skill or age, but by personal choice and belonging.

"I'll have Mikey."

Then he eagerly shuffles to my team.

"I'll have Gary," strengthens the opposition.

"Paul."

"Jimmy."

"Andy."

On and on, names and faces changing with the season of orgasmic summers when participants declared other interest none-too-innocent or unbridled.

"Hop scotch, full stop, ques-tion-mark," laid out in bounding leaps before a face turning catch-out. Everyone was "It" for delirious spells of disease: not the "It" of plagued fashion, gnawing at hems, tugging for recognition, insatiable for the crocked half-life of stardom. We were all heroes hiding from time, in pursuit of another face, turned around by coattail, a tornado of exuberance clearing the cobwebs from Manic Street. Like arcade amusements where claws touch but do not arrest the novelties sweated together by hungry hands, we skirted passed preachers hanging out philosophies which rested as fragments in our uncultivated subconscious.

We were ageless in our happiness, scuffed and bruised by the glory of being a part of apparently infinite action, unaware of the growing that would throw us up into a present, suspended at crossroads of the decapitated hooks we were seemingly endlessly tethered to, that dripped one blood cell of experience to overwhelm us with question marks.

From there, the prosaic procession of memories built on accumulation, all too suddenly attentive to the necessities of direction; the sucking call of meaning drained of innocence. Without the fanfare of loss, childhood was cordoned off, merely a museum piece to draw on as we disseminated the fractures of preachers' words we had once so effortlessly breezed through.

Returning inwards, to my ancestral home, where there is no surface, just feeling, I am forced back to the present by the upheaval of a heartbeat rhythm quickened by the imperatives of facing the future. Left of centre, there is a beat to suggest waking, the tentative beginnings of something new, something not yet free from guilt: "It makes me angry, ashamed, but really alive." There is a questing of the shedding skin, the catharsis that has cleansed the soul, but at "what price?" There's a mixture of anger, despondency and a need to convince in "What's the point in always looking back/When all you see is more and more junk?" This is a renewal wracked with doubt, but the lurching breathing, emerging from a pool of reminiscence, is determined to leave the old self behind, the voice not wanting to look back and drown in the garbage of poisonous poignancy. What is beginning is not yet tangible or definable, but it has feeling, it has soul. It's the hesitancy of "Maybe" of "Seems" of "I only wish it was the truth." The sounds are pulling free, the effort wearying and still tied up in guilt and conscience, but winter will bring hibernation and the dreams that may ignite at some future point.

"No more bosses versus workers," announced Tony Blair, with safe-seat applause drowning out the irony of industrious sounds, bleeding, nailing shut Liverpool Dockers' coffins.

"No more bosses versus workers," said George Lewis, with an abrasively coughed laugh to mock.

"Of course, we agree, we have no choice. When a boss puts a gun to your head and threatens the sack, there is no fight to be employed. Yes, Mr Blair, there's not going to be any more embarrassing headlines in *The Daily Mail* about those troublesome working people and their troublesome unions causing a fuss about being ordered to eat shit by bosses. We'll clean the faecal bowl with a smile."

I left town late autumn, by some measure not filling up the white van Mikey had hired. The preachers were out, wishing "all the best" during a laboured departure. Passed empty homes slapped with the condemnation of posters, overwhelming those still living in meek light, I noticed busyness in the movements of those also readying themselves for moving. It was inevitable now, and I felt some guilt, but more prominent was a sense of relief that I wouldn't be around when wrecking crews moved in.

Captured by photographer Kevin Carter, the image of a dying child in Rwanda, helplessly fading where economies could not flourish. We may ache with the sadness of being voyeuristic participants in this shame, but dominant in the photograph is the waiting vulture that couldn't give a fuck for negotiations and the mealy-mouthed organisation of relief. Ready to pick bones for its own young ones huddled somewhere in the eyesore of aridness where conscience has no pop promo, nor star names attached.

9
THE MASSES

May 1st 1997 seems like a new dawn as the Tories get kicked out. Blair and Britpop are seemingly a breath of fresh air, but in the less than fresh air of the Labour Social Club, there existed only meagre exhilaration.

The organ player milks it, George Lewis churning out his cheesy tunes for the mouldy oldies whose movements are unexpected for their stiffened bodies, bringing a pool of tears to their eyes, ready to be rocked out as nostalgia comes calling. In their eyes, the organ player sees reflections; of a world he once knew, when good times chimed with glasses and living could be felt in the bodies that mingled. Life had a different perspective then – not necessarily 'rose-tinted' – but somehow more invigorating.

He could play the tune without concentration, could detach his soul from the performance, detaching his thoughts from a scene he had become set in. Occasionally, his eyes moved about the room, as a kind of check, abbreviating the moment to a blur of fading flesh.

Collective experiences were connecting, remembering a place, a world, even a universe where their existence had a foothold. It was a muted scream from a merged past. A flicker of recognition, a snapshot of history, a blink to remember, and then a blink to forget; all lead to an overwhelming question. Drowning, drowning, and drowning in mediocrity.

But his sounds threw them a lifeline, caught them before they fell back up the cliff.

They were back in the dry fields chasing a dream.

The organ player felt himself receding into the background; a place where his life's summary seemed to place him, albeit with his influence thinning. They were too engaged to remember the catalyst and he felt nondescript. The repetition stimulated

161

recollection like an inconsequential indifference. They were there and he was here, and departing. They were drinking up, but always in touch with the sobriety of tomorrow, when Manic Street was to be demolished and they would be finally anchored in their new, disparate homes. No longer with tangible histories, they would be condemned to face the grave and spend days totting up the numbers of final solutions.

They cheered vigorously when another Tory lost a seat, when the flaccid swing-o-meter blushed as it touched deeper into working class glory.

"Oh, we'll be alright now," mocked Mrs Maines. "We'd better start packing again to move back home."

They all laughed, pulling gristle from the autopsy.

"I'll get my old mining tools out too, eh?" added Dickie Chadwick. "Blair will be re-opening the mines in the morning for us poor folk."

They were locked in passed midnight, coated in the black humour of a buried world, working as one to mock the Conservative defeat and the blind euphoria of change. Eyes rolling, bodies sagging, they departed in drips, catching taxis to separate places, taking morsels of warmth to furnish unsentimentally new homes.

Danny Madison was let in to a welcome, enthusiastically recognised as the town's new Member of Parliament, taking back slaps and cheers without the artifice of sentimentality.

"Well done Danny," said Tommy Madden. "You'll do us proud. Those bastard Tories are going, going, gone!"

"Eighteen years of misery have ended tonight," he announced as drinks were pushed in front of him. "I wish Bill Harris could have been here, but in his absence, let's raise a glass to the man. He's laughing up there right now!"

George, Pete, Dickie and Ray played on until their sounds could no longer keep pace, disintegrating into a hearty cacophony of gleeful obscenities.

"They're saying Portillo's seat's in danger," drew all towards the television screen for an unbridled conclusion to the night.

Rousing chants raised the red flag on conquered ground before guts spilled out into familiar lamplight to find a way home through foreign avenues.

Demolition began early, as if those mapping out the splendour of proposed new homes were intent that it should be done most surreptitiously. Despite this, a crowd had gathered before the first wrecking ball blasted. Men without employment and a rabble of wives and grandchildren were there to pick from the debris some memory-bones. They were tears and spasms of defiance, coalescing in splutters to mark the amputation of time. A pulverising process continued throughout the day, and as some went home, others joined, leaving work without dinner to watch over the destruction.

"It doesn't take 'em long to knock 'em down," said George. "I see my place is still standing."

"I reckon they're keeping it as a sort of shrine, George," Pete Thornby joked. "They'll be charging the middle classes to come and look around one day, just to see how us simple folks lived."

"'Course, they'll have to fix in a pigeon shack, maybe sculpt some stone whippets, 'cos I sort of missed them out when they designed me."

"Aye, it'll be the next Beamish. Maybe Tony Blair could come up and cut a ribbon."

"In between cutting throats."

Grim badinage served to disguise defeatism as they observed the silence of machines employed to destroy. An ejaculation of rubble truncated the street, exhausted dust shifted by gusts revealing emaciated architecture. The shells of houses still standing were mockingly alive with the anguished ache of timber and falling mortar, contracting limply in parody of scrotal temperature maintenance. Particle puffs spew into wombless air, scattering impotent rage, rupturing the purity of oxygen, weighted to fall on other desolate, insensitive spots around town where back street abortions de-generate spaces.

During the night, unknown forces, playful Decadent Marxists, smashed the windows of resting machines and delayed destruction for half a day. In response, the wreckers positioned a cabin where once a house functioned, and placed in it a security guard who'd never lived in town.

Those who once dwelt returned most days, and there was a bathetic necessity in the desire to be witness to one's former home being bruised into submission. It took less than a week for the whole street to be levelled. After that, they were no more onlookers other than restless kids picking at scraps for souvenirs left stuck in unexplored cavities and those stopping off on a journey to some other place.

Stu, Natalie and Jenny paused to ignite cigarettes.

"There's childhood gone," said Stu. "The capitalists have won. They'll be chasing us off this street next year for bringing the tone of the neighbourhood down."

"Nostalgia is a drug, a disease, a placebo for the poor. I'm not going to indulge," said Natalie. "We're still together, and our new place is okay. I haven't been abused or chased by townies, yet."

"Come on, I don't wanna stay," said Jenny.

They meandered towards the beach, noticing that the bench they had carved into life over years had been uprooted and taken away. All along the sea front path, the benches had been pounded from moorings, leaving shattered spots awaiting renewal.

"They've got something against us three, haven't they?" concluded Stu, his humoured blackened by sarcasm of septic opportunities.

At least the cave hadn't been renovated, still gloriously daubed with words and etchings from their past. None had brought equipment to add to the anarchic Art, content instead to sit in smoky skins, rocking on stones and teetering on their futures.

"We got the list of books we'll be studying at college," said Natalie, speaking for Stu as both would be attending the same place. "Jane fucking Austen for god's sake! That leaves me cold."

"And Congreve too," added Stu. "We'll be foppish dandies by the end of the course. But Hardy's okay, and Coleridge liked his opium and gothic imagery. Have you got your list yet, Jenny?"

"No, but I'm sure it'll be pretty similar. Hey, it's only a short walk between our colleges. We'll have to meet up at dinner time."

"Definitely," said Natalie.

"I'm going to be critical of the shitty texts, that'll be a laugh. It'll be Charles Bukowski taking Jane Austen out for a drink, then fucking her up her tight ass."

"You look at these walls and see how many years we've been coming here, and how quickly time has passed," said Jenny. "Two years will go very fast, then what?"

"University, I suppose," replied Natalie.

"I'm going to University," said Stu. "I can't wait to get away from the dickheads living their dickhead lives, who know nothing of books and learning, whose fear of difference makes them drunk and violent." He added, "but we'll all stay together," as a postscript.

"It's a town full of strangers now. Before, even on Manic Street, when they were people you barely talked to, you were at least reassured by their continued presence," said Natalie. "I know we'll stay friends for ever, but we'll be less cohesive, like the town itself I suppose."

"It's a town haunted by the past, that's all," interrupted Stu, feverishly inhaling a cigarette to the filter. "Don't get dewy-eyed about it, Nat. We're at a dead end here. We always said we'd leave as soon as possible. I can't fuckin' wait."

"But whatever we are, we are like this because of our environment, you can't deny that," said Jenny.

"Not as much as some might think," argued Stu. "If it were the case, how come I'm not rushing into a job and spending my weekends drinking myself into the gutter, chasing women only for sex? No, this environment didn't prompt me to read *The Catcher In The Rye*, listen to The Velvet Underground and dress the way I am. How many of the lads and ladettes parading their self-absorption round pubs and clubs ever stop to think and question and challenge what they've become? No, fuck this environment, it is so cold dead."

"That's rubbish, Stu," replied Natalie. "You've become who you are because there was something to kick against. And by the way, it's fucking easy for us to be outsiders and self-proclaimed intellectuals when we've been handed the tools for improvement. You've got a home, Stu. You might not be rich, but you're not homeless or in poverty. You've had the time to grow as you wish. We're all living a reasonably comfortable life where we don't have to even think about a need to earn money right now."

An argument wedged into the separation each one had long felt opening throughout a summer of post-exam boredom and inconclusive self-contemplation. Blame found no escape in the lives they were now equipped but reluctant to embark on, so they turned inward, cantankerous amid the impossibility of answers. Though they parted with the perfunctory seal of hugs and kisses, they were cool with a resentment slipping between the pores of undying love.

Before their courses started, they were once again united in furiously cogent argument, excitedly conversing and daubing their cave the evening after Princess Diana died.

"Me mam hasn't turned off the telly all day," said Natalie. "I can't believe it, but she was actually crying at one stage. It's like she's lost a relative or something."

"Our mam is the same," added Jenny. "I don't get it. Some airhead woman dies in a crash. It's sad that she died, because she's got two kids, and she wasn't some evil bitch or anything, but our house has always been against the royals, and now they're acting like it's the end of the world."

"I'm totally unmoved," said Stu. "She had a life of riches, parading fashions around the world, playing the media game and enjoying it. Oh, they talk about her charity work and weep and weep, but if she was so fuckin' charitable why didn't she donate some of her money?"

"Yeh, it's a tough life being a royal. Fuck her, speeding around the streets with her playboy boyfriend. Everyone's blaming the press for chasing her around, but hang on, how many newspapers, magazines and television programmes has she given her time to? She wasn't screeching off into the night then, was she?"

Stu spoke the words he was spraying: "Thirtieth of August nineteen ninety-seven. Still starving in third world countries, still genocide on our Earth and some blonde Princess or other carps it."

For the following week, there was a unity of grief, flabby with tears, perceptible around the kingdom. Junkies put down syringes for one-eyed salutes, hungry bellies were nourished on the maudlin guidance of television rapists and stocks of patriotism were priced up and sold off with the totems of Korean-made Union Jacks. The literature of signatures filled books where intellectual commitment was not required as masses of nobodies staked a claim to significance.

Labour Party rats had paged Danny Madison, insisting he cancel all engagements, but Danny felt compelled to still attend a long scheduled meeting organising further support for the Liverpool Dockers. It was indebted to a lower key than expected, devoid of speeches, merely concerned with assigning paper tasks to the supporters' group, before resting in sombre exchanges.

"She doesn't mean anything to me," said Tommy Madden. "Tony Blair calls her the People's Princess, well, that might be true for the chattering classes and media mouthpieces, but she wasn't my princess. This bloody grieving is the establishment laughing at the people, telling us all that the deaths of ordinary people aren't as important as hers. Bill Harris did more for people during his life time than she ever came close to."

"Look, I'm not into knocking Tony Blair for the sake of it," said Danny. "That's the Tory press thing to do. Even if he is more Right wing than any Labour leader in history, he's still not Tory, and they don't like it. There's a programme for investment in schools and hospitals that the Tories would never countenance. However, like you say, this week has been a bit over the top. You know, Blair didn't come up with that 'People's Princess' thing. His spin doctors composed it, and it somehow rings hollow when you know the whole things been so stage managed."

"Here's a fact you won't see on the news for a while," announced George. "Diana had an estimated fortune of forty million pounds. Why didn't any of that reach her beloved charities?"

"The whole things a facade," said Ray. "If you can't stir up a war to unite the people, then manufactured tragedy will do the job just as well. No one's talking about Iraqi children dying daily because of Western sanctions. Isn't this a bigger tragedy? Two princes have lost a mother. Well, yes, I can still feel sad about that, but it's their personal tragedy and it shouldn't be forced on others. In Iraq, mothers, fathers and children die each day, and bloody hell, we could stop it if we wanted to! Put this to most politicians and they'll tell you it's about getting rid of Saddam Hussein, but how come he was left there after the war?" Ray paused, aroused by truths he had garnered from continued studying of post-war developments. "There was an uprising after the war, in Southern Iraq, and it might've got rid of Hussein if America had backed it, but they didn't. Instead, they allowed Hussein to brutally quell the uprising. Sorry Danny, you aside, most politicians are liars and opportunists. In the media age they are savvy enough to know how to create a good smokescreen and delude the people."

"Well, the Dockers are going to get even less press aren't they?" said George. "I'm sure we'll be burying Diana for a few months yet."

"You're right," acknowledged Danny, "but the fight goes on, that's what matters."

Man of the people, the Dockers' Union Leader, Bill Morris, threw wreaths for the workers with platitudes purchased from fast-buck spivs operating on streets brimming with malleable souvenir-hunters. At the TGWU's conference he wore the Tory dress of law and order and insisted that a vote to support the Dockers had been defeated. But, with the floor in uproar, a second ballot won the vote and cheered for old values edited from the carefully scripted proceedings. Morris, in the headlights of rushing old blood, still refused to back the Dockers. Instead, he made inaccurate claims that he had written to the government asking it to intervene in the dispute. No such request had been received, and the Dockers were left outside the conference, shaking buckets for bread, looking to winter without their union's backing.

Diana's forty million pounds of assets bought her a carnival funeral, whilst the Dockers existed on the twelve pounds a week their union grudgingly gave them.

"If the union had made the strike official they would have got three times as much," said George, rattling a collection at the social club. "They're being starved into submission. The battle is coming to an end, but the fight is recorded in history to embarrass all those involved who did nothing. Shame on you Tony Blair, shame on you Bill Morris. I salute the men, women and children and the nobility of their fight."

Construction work had started on Manic Street before the year was out, halted at intervals by the belligerence of youth. Christmas was celebrated at far away places around town, old residents stuffed into their new homes and unmolested by the comfort of neighbours. They gathered at the social club, their numbers decayed, prudent in their indulgence, keeping a bit back for costs involved in returning home.

Ray Young heaved into the grave before the cruelty of spring, believing in God during his last hours, dwelling on fondly remembered moments through the creases of old photographs, and sure he would meet John somewhere beyond flesh.

George, Dickie and Pete reorganised the band with George taking lead vocals for a while. He didn't have the sweeping range of Ray's voice, so they worked through simple rock numbers to rattle the bones of the club. When Pete died not long after, the two other band members had little heart to continue. Club regulars would keep asking them when they were going to return, and they were persuaded to audition for a new drummer. On the two occasions they found replacements, each was young, fired by contemporary vigour and just passing through. More compelling for George and Dickie was unease at seeking to fill the spaces where their friends had been for boundless years.

169

The option to continue as a two-piece involved Dickie re-familiarising himself with lead guitar and hiring a machine to fill the other sounds. Neither they nor the club could afford to hire the contraption indefinitely, so a chart was pinned to the wall and a fund set up to raise money to one day buy the necessary apparatus. Whilst it accumulated – every now and then dipped into for a cause or a charity – someone brought in a hi-fi and there was meagre contentment in boozy sing-along and Dickie's occasional rehearsals.

Marcus Bowles dragged local reporters to the site where fabulous quarters were being erected, gushing his acumen all over the business pages. No longer was there talk of affordable housing:

"This is the beginning of a new town. These modern apartments will attract businessman to the town, to invest where once there was only decay. People talk about how sad it is that this old street is gone, but I lived here once, and let me tell you, the houses may have been fine for fifty years ago, but time moves on and there will only be a re-birth when change is allowed."

During their first year at college, Natalie, Jenny and Stu were less frequent in visiting the cave. They bruised books they were studying and argued with the same intellectual ferocity when disseminating the prevailing culture, and for a while they still met up at secluded spots during breaks. Yet, with each revolution they were drifting further apart, subtly shedding skins and barely solidified by a unity that atrophied in reflections alien to their present. Sometimes only two would meet up and soon give up, untouched by anecdotes intruding on their own. They were anchored by partners, fluid with emotions, and slightly embarrassed by the curiosity of old bonds.

With full-time employment in London, I had little time to return to my birth place, choosing instead to visit Mikey and receive second-hand updates on what was happening after he'd been up to see what was left of his friends. However, over the summer, I went back with Mikey to stay a few days at Danny Madison's.

Whilst Mikey borrowed a bike for expansive rejuvenation, I dawdled to spots for snapshots of old, desperate for the humdrum architecture that might offer reattachment. Blasphemous on sore ground, I could not dwell at Manic Street, now no longer even commemorated with the symbolic life support of a signpost. Fabulous erections merely echoed the stapled stares of centrefold capitalization, skinned of affection, desultory in their potency. Instead of the fevered dialogue of preachers, there was the furtive murmur of machines punctuated by statistical communication choking the means to an end.

Some of the frivolous businesses symphonic in money-drops were still washing in and washing out the bored kids and pensioners, although clients were now more elusive, losing pensions and giros and taxing themselves submissively with the airless optimism of a National Lottery.

No longer did I feel the regurgitated lament of innocence lost, instead struck aggressively by lives clicking for digits that would change the anaemic predictability of tomorrows, lacerating routines of diminishing options, clawing at futures resisting their desperate advances and only willing to teach the loneliness of knowing your place. The present, a conveyor belt of brutality, nailed lives shut with a lesson to be afraid.

These preacher-less streets were a victory for political passivity, emblematic of the historical amnesia prevalent in contemporary society, one willing to forget the rise of fascism, its evils and the lessons that should have been learned, one rather keener to ignore through an incantation of "keep my head down." Materialism buys seclusion and pacifism sometimes doesn't work, but the sybaritic vagrants of the new world order are complicit by their ignorance. Racist slogans stain empty facades on the sea front where revellers gather in spastic dances saluting national pride. Though they may tut tut at the machine gun's butt, they are too blissful with modernity to look back at a holocaust running through all skins and bloods. Dying for greater freedom and justice offers no tastes to palates busy with consumption and expulsions and the hazy anecdotes of riotous indiscretion.

There are no heroes or heroines to put a spoke in middle class comfort, or challenge their apathy, or indeed their toleration of things. In the wider world, dictators are killing innocents with weapons supplied by our government. This town and the bodies therein, mirrored in the factory-farmed politics spinning across the land, are content to withdraw from analysis, revelling in media-warped synthetics, hoping for scraps from the famous. Participation is the essential in lives uncomplicated by meaning. Whilst old men are humoured as they talk of "glory days" not filmed or photographed, a backward generation eagerly seeks to be present at whatever event is currently the Big Thing, or else be narcotic in antiquities where tu'penny ha'penny sound bites glorify their youth.

"I was there when the television cameras rolled, and I have been taught memories by celebrity prompts. I signed the book of condolence when Diana dried up, and I was there when we marched for McDonald's latest cause. Here is a photograph of us in the crowd, here is a memento overpriced at the time. I've squeezed into the frame where disease and war are a virginal backdrop, got my smiles indented upon history's shadow."

No one really wants to hear George Lewis saying, "I used to work at the mine over there."

"Were there any celebrities there?" is the only thing that gives significance. "Did they do a programme on it? Y'know, like *Top Ten Industrial Disputes*, counted down to a pop parade of ephemera. Or maybe, you know, let's just think outside the box. What about, a top ten pits who held out the longest? We could have miners telling us about what was on TV at the time, combining their words with music that sound tracked their struggle. Or even, top ten post-Thatcher industrial black spots, make it a bit jokey, have a look at all those poor miners working as shop assistants, telesales people, and security guards. It's been years now; we can all laugh about it."

Midweek, me, Mikey and Danny went to the old social club. The regulars were mostly absent, waiting until the weekend to gather. Most of the talk was idle, barring a few people challenging Danny over what Tony Blair was doing for the country. George

Lewis was more intent to talk about the fund to buy a music programmer so he and Dickie could play again. Mikey and I, in the comfort zone of employment, chipped in, prompting a unity of purpose and applause when the appeal chart, withered on the wall, was coloured by a red pencil pock-marked by ruminations, ascending breathless red to almost touching distance of the summit.

Truth is, I was glad to get away from my hometown, the short stay weighing me down with an untouchable past, leaving me feeling guilty and sad. A gap had opened between whatever it was that enabled my parents to flourish and what now held sway in the town's circulation.

"Pathetic acts for a worthless cause," chimed preachers from disparate pulpits, unable to find the fluidity of purpose when their Labour government offered nothing but the patronising smiles of old glories repackaged. The lip service of a kiss-off, scattered on rubble, left ambition destitute and gave excuse for forcing onto working classes a new, toothless design for life. I didn't have answer or antidote, embarrassed by my inability to reciprocate when the preachers found fossil fuels to articulate a perpetual struggle in inexorable decay.

"It's our party, and it always will be," said George. "They can call it New Labour, or whatever name tots up votes from comfortable homes, but it's still a Labour Party, and it's still the party of the people. We now have to fight from within. If there are still people like Tony Benn and Dennis Skinner in the party, then it must still be our party, so we haven't been cut loose just yet." But "we still have a choice, we still have the vote," offers only hollow affirmation when the creeping neutrality of middle-thinking practicality dilutes all opposition who question the soothing political current of Blair's leadership.

All that seems to exist is the second-hand misery of history, trawled through for a meaning, which might feed wisdom into the dead-end of a present. Danny Bertram works a taxi and drives around heart-attack hours, matching up ungainly snippets he's pieced together from the labour of ages and the tittle-tattle of journeys:

"Did you know, we stood side by side at the pit entrance, stood up to the government in numbers greater than thousands, and we were strong and determined and unified by justice. You've seen those clips on TV, haven't you, when all those miners were battling the police? Yeh, I was one of them, and me brothers too. And y'know, over there, that was once our street, where everyone knew their neighbour, not just next door, but neighbours any door down. It's not there anymore, but we still care. We do. We still care. These things won't be forgotten."

"Just here's fine, thanks," drops off an audience before Bertram beats around clotted spots for another fare of blank-eyed witnesses.

"We're not ready for drowning, not my far away comrades or me. And do you know what; we've been selling weapons to countries like Indonesia, so they can drop bombs on the unreported people of East Timor. There's no end to the brutality acted out around this connected globe, and we are the bystanders who'll let it happen again and again. They once flooded a Welsh village in the nineteen fifties just to supply water to Liverpool, and now we look back with synthetic anger at the untouchable aftermath of histories. *They*, is the big spinning them, the intangibility of expedient power, grinding through its machinations as we sleep, condemning their dishonesty to history as we grasp for audible dexterity elegant enough to escape the pissing-on cockiness of middle class sarcasm. When we wake, it's too late because the fight will always be playing catch up. You blink at dawn and it's gone. The pit is gone, the activist is silenced. A tsunami of conscience is broken up and shattered and we are imprisoned by sheer silence."

"This house, just here. How much is that?"

Bertram cranks up a figure and loses a thread in departures.

"Looks like you've had a good night lads? If you're gonna be sick, just give us a shout and I'll pull over. Oh, you're off to the match this weekend? Do you remember that semi-final at Hillsborough? Yeh that kind of thing shouldn't happen at a football match. Of course, no one's to blame when ordinary people die. What about the police then? Look at the truth and you can see it was them that made it happen, directing people into suffocating cages. Remember *The Sun* newspaper telling all those lies about Liverpool fans stealing from dead souls' pockets and pissing on corpses? Pack of lies, and proven to be such, but there's been no apology has there? Y'know what, it restores my faith that in Liverpool, hardly anyone buys *The Sun*. Oh, right here? Okay. That's five pounds fifty, please."

Memory has become a pain, bruised into submission, carried as crosses by all those still living routines around town. Danny Bertram began to die doing a late night shift, took his pain home for a final act in front of his wife. Rushed to a hospital, he was gone before arrival, prompting an emotion of motions pitter-pattering towards conclusions.

The last year of old numbers, marked on religion's scattergun calendar, saw further departures from town as old Manic Street became habitable once more. Sleek designs were stuffed with interested monies; the elegant erections offering ocean views for the nonchalant. None of the previous inhabitants could afford a new house on Manic Street, and so they suffocated a past with chattering about materialism and percentages.

Natalie, Jenny and Stu laboured through emotions, clogged up in their cave with sea changes in their blood. They laughed at their spirits and presumed coalescence would be natural, but each one somehow knew this was a last dash into their adolescence to plunder parts worthy of the future. They were going to universities, preparing for journeys by rail, bus and mule, and they were only vague about any need to return to their birth. They loved each other in words and in actions, but they were lasciviously potent to taste articulations that would move body and soul further and further away.

"I'm gonna take my imagination to detonate at new places," said Stu. "I'm gonna take my poorly spoken anger and explode dirty bombs at comfort zones. These are my thoughts and they will always be mine, secluded with skull, wired up at the edges, and readied to imagine the darkest of images: No government can touch it, no law can

175

constrain it. There is no morality in my head, just a happy Hell of tyrannies where rapists run amuck and make laws for themselves."

Around town, you could blot out the numbers of lives still kicking with passion like you'd fill in lottery possibilities. George and Dickie mastered the machine that could fashion old tunes and played along to them with vocals and lead guitar in karaoke approximations. It thrilled the few who still gathered by tearing their existence from retirement and dribbling the preachings that few could muster sufficient imagination to make tangible.

The old millennium was sung out, rhythmic in withered, calloused, swinging hands, for old lands sighing last breaths hoarse with new horizons. The new flailed the flesh from pasts stuck between gravestones and glorious nostalgia to force on incorporeal fashions only sensitive to capitulation by proxy. Manic Street in Manic Town and across many manic limbs had to be gluttonous on the promises of tomorrows indifferent to calendar movements.

"All the best," rattled out in the social club and coursed through the limbs of fair nations, and left us with a headache of unassailability in the cold malevolence of impending days where thoughts would seep in and dilute whatever plans were previously potent.

A song for the new era came as *The Masses Against The* Classes: a thunderous fit of a return to form for the Manic Street Preachers, engaged with a sample from left wing dissent Noam Chomsky preceding rushing guitars and political spitting: "Hello, it's us again/We're still so in love with you," knowingly alerts the listener to an awareness of the possibility of slipping into self-parody, whilst the reference to *You Love Us* is meant to signal that the same fire that once burned is still present: "Yes, we mean it too." There's a confidence in the driving rhythms, an army of revolutionaries rising over hills to stream down into the centre of power, a unity of feeling that chimes in with the thriving anti-globalisation movement.

We are no longer few and we have righteousness and justice, reason and humanity on our side. Kicking over tables and scattering the coins and notes, this is a flood of possibilities.

"Can you feel it like it was before?" seeks to rip open the complacency that is symptomatic of the middle classes, comfortable under New Labour. Perhaps there is even – in all the tongue in cheek lyricism – a sense of rejecting the overblown indulgence of the last album. This is the "for real" ethos re-stated, offering unconditional love and willingly laying bare so that the cynicism and hate of others can feed from the band, the parasitic press doing what they will, but the band no longer offering reason.

George Lewis and Dickie Chadwick don't feel the same, stuck in an endless loop of recycled pop from a bygone era, hobbling through tunes that once fed the rhythms of their lives. No new stimulus from ancient waves giving and receiving positive and negative in the spectral spray shuffling into alleys and streets deficient of imagination.

"There's nothing for the kids to do around here, so they drag around nooses in belligerent groups, tottering on street corners with recreational antagonism, incarcerated by circumstances they have grown to accept," said Danny Madison to an extract of committee. "We're looking to use some of the budget to build a youth centre on the sea front where the old garage used to be. Okay, we're going to have some games machines, pool tables, table tennis and the like, but if we can build round the back too, on the high street where there used to be a store, we can also have a hall for drama classes. Then we can use the upstairs for creative workshops. I've spoken to a few people who'd be willing to give time to teach music lessons and art classes, so it's going to be a place where young people can learn new skills and find direction. Listen, these days we look at the young as some kind of autonomous state which we dare not enter, but they have potential if we can give them the tools to tap into it."

"It's a great idea, Danny, and I see that you've got sponsors to meet some of the costs, but it's still some way short of what we can afford. However, I recommend we accept it in principal pending further developments. At this stage, I think we can only work on converting the garage site because the recreational front will bring in money. At a later date we can then think about linking it to the high street building."

Such incomplete movements seeking a means to coordinate progress were haphazardly promoted around the body of town: transmitted to reach the many but invariably diluted by pragmatism so that when idealism by committee completed its journey to the fissures and sulci of receptive streets it floundered with fatigue and offered mere sound-bite hope.

Looking out of tightened doorways and letting in light through wooden frames, occupiers were baffled by the invisibility of glamorous initiatives trumpeted in the press. No one blamed Danny Madison, who was always reluctant to shake a hand for photo opportunities, well aware such superficiality just patronised those bruised by disappointments, cognizant of the vacuity of political promises.

"It's a shame Danny," said George. "But don't give up, son. Dickie and me will still be here when you get the centre complete, and we'll still be willing to do some teaching. Truth is, we go through the motions most weekends, banging out old tunes and labouring through whatever forgettable ditty is clogging the charts. We knew it would never be the same without Ray and Pete, and yes, we do still get a kick out of the way the old crowd cheers us on, but it's a bit of a routine now, and with the machine we have to concentrate to keep up. We used to go with the rhythm, jam to our moods, y'know. When we were a band, we moved with the crowd, changed things, and had what they call soul. Now, we just perform and have to flick buttons to pause a machine so we can indulge in some banter. Then, it's back to the routine. We're getting too old for it. I'd love to get some youngsters playing in there. Y'know, a lot of them love the old songs too. Well, they pick 'em up from the adverts don't they? Still, we don't give up hope."

Strangers settling in town outnumbered the preachers. People too busy to pass the time in communication would not hear their voices. When Christmas came, the decorations were cast out earlier; more widespread and more cluttered, signalling attempts to be a part of the televised party through purchasing the moment. A desire to be looked on had nothing to do with sharing, but rather to be noted as participating for a half-limelight of fame. This was a society gluttonous for a material past, worshipping the totems of from where it came. Remembering eras where innocence always had to fit into fashions and fads, you could not find the oxygen of memories if your anecdote didn't chime with some talking head puking up recollections cleansed by materialism. How we used to live offers artificial endorphins to make us forget the present, soothing us so we grow complacent of slaughter. If you didn't have one of the top ten Christmas toys, your existence is an accumulation of nothing. Around the calendar's corner, there is saviour in more lists reeking with celebrities endorsing selective amnesia. An irresistible retreat into the recent past grows fatter in numerous countdowns when top ten becomes top fifty, and then top hundred, so that many more can be drugged into participation.

Television amputation will make us all perfect in design; with our waking senses functioning along lines re-shaped on ageing faces to wear the scars of profit and loss. For youth, most potent is the disillusionment of separation, at not being able to keep up with the fashions of peers. Festering resentment spits out defiance from born again preacher-kids:

"I don't fuckin' care, they can shove it up their arse."

Dickie Chadwick's fighting cancer from the pit of his belly, locked away with bass strings and topped up on cranberry juice. Friends and relatives wait for buses to see him, falling into an ocean where pain is dissipated, unified in yearnings moored to the preciousness of life. He died that September and did not wake to the fever of terrorism pornographic on screens.

"Who would want to do something like that? Flying planes into buildings? I just don't understand it. Who would want to do that?"

"What about all the people and countries America has tortured and bombed in the past?" offered George Lewis, moving away from the crematorium. "American governments have been the biggest sponsors of terrorism for the last fifty years, and I could spend all day giving you a list with the authority of truth. But, I can't be bothered.

Show me the man who's going to blow up the White House and I'll shake his hand. Do you think I care about President Bush? He can go to hell with his dad. All those people who died today are the victims of American terrorism as much as the people of Vietnam, Nicaragua, El Salvador..."

Echoes bark, burrowing into retreating rings, which mark at intervals the solid mass of all that was once dignified by the substance of being consequential. Worming into memory, making a disease of history: non-communication or obfuscation, making obsolete any preachers with a will to articulate. Defeatism offers some senses-bludgeoned optimism, or at least that is the forced conclusion from raging flames of frames still knotting together vocabulary.

"How do you think it feels to be like me?" asks Mohammed Khan, bloodying his fingerprints on shards of broken glass. "I've lived in this town for over twenty years. You know, I've had the same trials and tribulations as anyone, worrying for my family and my community, but you can add to that the racism that has always existed. You know what? I don't have a god, but I've still had my family spat at and abused in the name of religion. What kind of god wants to fill heaven with corpses? If death is so noble, why don't the leaders detonate their bodies for Allah? I can't tell this to cretins who hate me for my skin. They've won. I'm not going to fix up this shop again, not going to wash away diseased words that turn me inside out. Fuck all religions and fuck all ideologies, they're for the selfish and deeply unimaginative."

"Yah fuckin' Paki!" misrepresents Mohammed in so many ways. But listen to this man. Though he is not a preacher – he has no faith in humanity he is not evolved enough to join – his words find reception amongst those living on infected streets. "You lot are all terrorists, sick bastards blowing yourself up. Your lot and fuckin' Saddam Hussein are all evil terrorists. And another thing, those fuckin' immigrants, bloody niggers and Pakis and Arabs, they come over to this country to get our benefits, then they fuckin' blow up our women and children." Joe is one of the new money people living on Manic Street, pure-Thatcherite and self-proclaimed "ordinary, working man." He's a racist cunt, and that's all the words any onlooker need administer to inflate his otherwise nondescript being.

You can still find some semblance of sanity about town, from a preacher not yet willing to turn out the light, or one passing through on return.

Language ghost whores leave abrasions across desolate streets, where slabs cover flabby rhetoric for red carpet non-entities:

"You see them on the television, vacuuming up celebrity, spunking up their souls for dissection by media," says Natalie Maines. "They are disembowelled of reason, sucking up to fame like it's an epiphany. They have no brains and a silent *Cunt* precedes their names. Cunt-Titmuss, Cunt-Jade, Cunt-Brian, Cunt-Lady-Cocksucker-Blues. You are all cunts perfectly formed for arsehole expulsion. You see them all, saturating cathode rays, puking on column inches, parading their ignorance, and willingly selling their idiocy and sluttishness for stretch-marked time in the limelight. You can slice off any part of my life, even the most mundane, banal moments ruminating on Manic Street, and it would still have more erudition and soul than the accumulation of their beings."

"All their come is absorbed by tabloids and printed for our pleasure," says Stu. "*The News Of The World* is an abortion of the senses, plopped out by monkeys masturbating without opposable thumbs. Then sold to the ignorant like a whack over the head, loosening brain cells to fall into the gutter. What's Pete Doherty then, but a smack head of excess? It's just too complex to write about genius when you're dribbling for decadence. There's no space in the Doherty-drama for passion and resistance, no dissemination of how music can electrify the soul. You know what, get me a passenger plane filled with tabloid hacks, and I'll fly it into number ten Downing Street so we can all get to nirvana."

"I am resigning from the party for the good of my conscience," Danny Madison tells a rattling congregation at the old social club. "This is not my Labour Party anymore. It's not our Labour Party. It's the party of spin, of knee-jerk opportunism, on-the-hoof policy making. What credibility has Tony Blair got when he can lie to the country and then smile and absolve himself with his imbecile's grin? He still sleeps well at night when thousands of innocents die in Iraq. Does he count the children dying daily because of his lying and folly? Or does he instead ponder how to extricate himself from the chaos and re-claim more votes? Blair and Bush are the real terrorists on Earth, too busy with mutual cocksucking to contemplate cause and effect. You know, in America I'd probably be arrested for this speech, probably taken to Guantanamo Bay to spend years incarcerated without trial. There is no conspiracy theory when I assert that George Bush Junior, alcoholic cretin, is a dictator and terrorist. You can't argue with it when he orders the killing of thousands of innocents not connected to any war or terrorist activity. It's a fact: a truly vile, brutal, stomach-churning fact. And then look at Blair: the empty-headed, lying cheerleader, a stain on the original principles of the Party. The way things are going; don't be surprised if words like these mean I am one day locked up. Honesty is going to be dangerous thing quite soon, if not already. No, this is not the Labour Party I once trusted. It's a phoney self-interested cabal of idiots and schemers."

George Lewis looked along the gleaming buildings on Manic Street, where no bodies were out preaching or joined in exchanges.

"Where are you now, the body and the soul? We will not see the like of these communities again, do you know that? People like me; we hardly dare talk about it, because our words are mocked as being old fashioned and clichéd. Down there, there used to be the kind of unity that made a difference. It was pure and righteous, and from door to door day in and day out, you could hear ideologies alive with protest and belief in social justice. Nah, I know, it's a joke isn't it? Why bother thinking about what you can do for your neighbour, when such time could be spent indulging the self? Well, we may die with few possessions and our media-unfriendly memories, but we pass on with souls rich with shared experiences and struggles. Sing it loud, sing it proud, we will be heard, we will be found."

INHALE AGAIN.